Leap Day

Leap Day

a novel by Wendy Mass

 LITTLE, BROWN AND COMPANY

New York ᷤ Boston

Also by Wendy Mass
A Mango-Shaped Space

Little, Brown and Company
Time Warner Book Group
1271 Avenue of the Americas, New York, NY 10020
Visit our Web site at www.lb-teens.com

First Edition

"Thirty days" poem (front flap) by Dan Beauvillia

Excerpt on self-esteem (page 102) reprinted from *Women and Self-Esteem,*
by Linda Tschirhart Sanford and Mary Ellen Donovan. First published in 1984
by Doubleday, a division of Random House.

Library of Congress Cataloging-in-Publication Data

Mass, Wendy.
Leap day : a novel / by Wendy Mass. — 1st ed.
p.   cm.
Summary: On her fourth Leap birthday, when she turns sixteen, Josie has a number
of momentous experiences, including taking her driver's test, auditioning for a
school play, and celebrating with her family and friends.
ISBN 0-316-53728-4
[1. Birthdays — Fiction.   2. Interpersonal relations — Fiction.   3. High schools —
Fiction.   4. Schools — Fiction.   5. Orlando (Fla.) — Fiction.]   I. Title.

PZ7.M42355Le 2004
[Fic] — dc22   2003054547

10   9   8   7   6   5   4

Q-FF

Printed in the United States of America

Book design by Billy Kelly
The text for this book was set in Gill Sans and Sabon MT, and the display type is Gill Sans Heavy

For EJ McCarthy and Debbie Stoler, who provided a summer of inspiration,

for Bob, Pat, and the french fry–eating squirrel at Drew University.

And with love to Mike, for sneaking in and making everything better

The real you is who you are when no one's watching.

Chapter IA: Josie

Right now it's seven o'clock on a Monday morning, and I'm lying on the floor of my bedroom watching the white plastic ceiling fan go around and around and around. I don't actually choose to sleep on the floor; some mornings I just wind up here. For the past few years I've had very vivid dreams, and I wind up flinging myself to the floor in the middle of the night. Now I keep a pillow by the side of the bed, so it's really not too bad. I feel safe on the floor. Like I'm more grounded. Sometimes I feel a bit untethered, like I'm more *on* the world than *in* it. I've always wanted to ask my friends if they feel like that, but I never do.

I sit up and rub the little crusts of yesterday's mascara out of my eyes. I can't hear the shower running, so Rob must still be sleeping. This is a good thing because it means I'll have all the hot water I need, and I need a lot. One time last year I turned on the water and then went back to my room for a second, and Rob ran into the shower. He screamed bloody murder and jumped out, hopping up and down on the fuzzy yellow bathmat. I ran in to see what all the fuss was about and got an eyeful. It's one thing to see your brother naked when you're five and he's seven, but it's another thing entirely when you're teenagers. I may be scarred for life. It's true that Rob and I get along better than any other brother and sister I know. But still, there are boundaries.

With the water just this side of scalding, I wash my hair twice. This is a big day for me, and one time just won't suffice. I haven't had a haircut in over a year, and now my hair falls right above my breasts. Speaking of my breasts, the left one is larger than the right. Only slightly, but it's bothered me ever since they started growing when I was twelve. I suppose it's possible that someone else might not be able to tell, but I can't be sure because no one else has ever seen them. Andrew Trachtenberg did touch them once over my sweatshirt behind the bleachers at the homecoming football game. After that his family moved away to one of the square-shaped states in the middle of the country. I try to tell myself that there's no connection.

So, technically, no one has actually seen them. Although that could change soon, considering I just turned sixteen — today, in fact — and I'm ready for a real boyfriend. So far I can't say that the first day of sixteen feels any different than the last day of fifteen. But I'm still very excited that it's my birthday. Especially since it's only my fourth one.

"Are you done yet?" Rob yells through the door. "I can't be late today. I have to meet with the coach before homeroom."

"Okay, okay, hold on." I push the old flowered shower curtain aside and reach for my towel, trying not to slip. Drying off takes me longer than I bet it takes most people, because I have a whole drying order that I like to follow that starts at my feet and winds up at my ears. When I'm done I wrap a smaller towel around my head like a fortune-teller. Then comes the citrus-scented oil, which I spray all over except for my chest, because I don't want to break out there. I don't think anyone can smell the oil through my clothes, but it makes me feel like I've got a secret. Then I throw on the purple bathrobe that my great-aunt sent me from New York. It's a little kid's bathrobe, and I think she meant to send it to my eleven-year-old cousin, but my mother won't let me return it since it fits fine. I try not to dwell on the fact that I look younger than I am. My mother is always trying to convince me that I have a very healthy body image for a teenager. Usually I would roll my eyes at something like that, but I think she really needs to believe it so I don't contradict her.

Rob knocks again. As soon as I open the door I hear, "Surprise!!!"

My parents and Rob are standing in the hall holding a homemade birthday corn muffin with a white candle stuck in it. A silver Mylar helium balloon waves at me from my doorknob. Below the HAPPY SWEET SIXTEEN message on the balloon, my mother has written in thick Magic Marker, "Happy Fourth Birthday to Our Favorite Leaper!" That's the name for people like me who were born on February 29th. Since leap year only comes around once every four years, that means that the 29th only exists once every four years. This took some getting used to. When I was five, Rob told me that my parents took my birthday away because I never went to sleep when I was supposed to. Nice. He then pointed to our kitchen calendar and showed me that the day was, in fact, not there. I cried for five straight hours until my mother explained the whole leap year thing to me. Then I cried for another five. Normally I celebrate my birthday on February 28th, but it never feels quite right. Now when February 29th does roll around, it's that much more special. Plus, we leapers are a pretty exclusive group. After all, there are 365 chances to be born on a regular day, but only a one-in-1,461 chance of having my birthday. In fact, I'm the only leaper at my high school.

I grin as they sing me the Happy Birthday song, and then Mom tells me to make a wish. This is only the first of many birthday things they'll do for me today to make up for all the ones I miss. I blow out the candle and wish that my breasts were the same size. Since I'll get to make many more wishes today, I don't mind wasting that one on something so shallow. I'll wish for world peace later.

"Happy birthday, sweetheart," Dad says, giving me a big hug. He's the more nurturing of my parents. Poor Dad. He's had a hard time of it lately. Six months ago his accounting firm merged with a bigger one and he was laid off. Now Mom's job catering parties is the only money coming in. Dad's been acting very secretive lately, and he hasn't been around for the past two weeks when I've come home from school. So either he has a lead on a new job or he's working undercover for the CIA, which is Rob's theory.

"Look in your room, Josie," Mom says, her eyes sparkling. My mother gets as excited about my Leap Day birthdays as I do. I think she's always felt a little guilty about the whole thing. "I tried to get you out a day earlier," she told me once. "The doctor suggested mixing castor oil and orange juice, but I just couldn't choke it down."

There is only one thing I want to find in my bedroom, and at first I don't see it. The first thing anyone would notice about my bedroom is the overwhelming pinkness of it. When I was ten I begged my mother to paint it pink. And not just any pink, but a hot, shocking pink. Since only two years before I had begged for — and received — the flowered wallpaper, she said all right to the pink paint, as long as I agreed not to ask for any more changes before college. At ten, college sounded a million miles away. So now I cringe every time I walk into my own room. Rob won't even come in at all. His room is a soothing army green. He says mine gives him a migraine. Even now he's hanging back in the doorway. I peer around the room, lift up the math book on my desk, open the top of my clothes hamper. Then my eyes fall on something sticking out from under the pillow on the floor. I toss the pillow aside and there it is. My very own key to Rob's car, which used to be Mom's car, which before that was Grandma's (my mom's mom, who passed away when I was ten), and which is now partly mine.

I literally squeal with delight and hold the key over my head like a prizewinner. I immediately put it on my new key chain so I won't lose it. The car is big and gray and has no left turn signal or air conditioning. We call it the Shark.

"You haven't passed the driver's test yet, Josie," Rob points out. "Lots of people fail the first time."

"Don't listen to him, honey," my mother says with a sideways glare at Rob. "You'll do just fine. You'd better get changed for school."

"I think you should wear the robe," Rob says as I close the door on him. Through the door he says, "You'll land the role of Juliet for sure if you wear it."

"I won't need any help," I reply, sounding much more certain than I am. To most people the school play is no big deal, but it is vital that I'm in it. Not only because I want to be a professional actress, but also because it's only when I'm on stage that I feel like I really affect people. In October, I finally got my first starring role. Mr. Polansky, the drama teacher, picked me to be Anna in the school's production of *The King and I*, and sophomores almost never get the lead in the fall musical. He said I was the best Anna he'd seen in years. Our school doesn't have much of a budget for the theater department, so we do *The King and I* every few years. That means he's seen a LOT of Annas. He's also seen a lot of Juliets. Even though it might not be fair to the others if he chose me again, I really want the part anyway. You can't call yourself an actress unless you've played Juliet. I love the heat of the spotlight, the smell of the makeup, the dusty old costumes that with only slight alterations get reused each year no matter what the play. Everyone pretending to be someone else, just for a night. It's so easy to know who to be when the words are right there on the page. I wish I found it so easy in real life. When I'm up there I feel connected to the world. It's some kind of cosmic joke that I have my driver's test and the play audition on the same day.

I yank my favorite jeans out of a drawer and lay them on the bed next to a red t-shirt that has THE FEW, THE PROUD, THE LEAPERS emblazoned in black letters. It's the motto of the NLA, the National Leapers Association. When I was eight, Mom registered me with the NLA. They pair you up with three other leapers born your same year. One of my leapmates, Chris from San Francisco, almost wasn't an official leaper. When he was born, his mother's doctor tried to get her to put either February 28 or March 1 on his birth certificate because it would be easier for him as he grew up. She refused.

Each Leap Day, my leapmates and I send each other gifts. So far this year I've gotten the t-shirt from Angela in Des Moines, a key chain with my name on it from Chris (with LEAP 2/29 on the other side), and I'm still awaiting my gift from Niki in Boston. She's the one I'm closest to, so I'm sure she'll send me something cool. I sent her a boxed set of the Winnie-the-Pooh books because she is a big Pooh fan (the *classic* Pooh, she is always quick to point out, not the distorted and too-bright Disney Pooh). I also sent her a Tori Amos CD that I knew she wanted. I sent Angela and Chris the CD too, and as a joke I sent them all caps from Disney World with Mickey Mouse ears and their names across the front. Oh, did I mention I live in Orlando, home of The Happiest Place on Earth?

At first my leapmates didn't believe that anyone actually lived in Orlando, but it's pretty much like living anywhere else. Except here, swarms of pale tourists can be found on every street corner, and by the time we graduate from high school everyone will have worked at one of the theme parks in some capacity. This summer I'm applying to be one of the face characters, preferably one of the nine Snow Whites at the Magic Kingdom. Since I have brown hair, I have a better shot at her than at Cinderella, who's blonde. There's a whole hierarchy to these jobs that most people don't know about. At the top are the actors who perform in the shows throughout the day. They sing and dance and get paid the most by far. Then there are the face characters who mingle with the guests, lip-sync in the parade, and sign autographs. Then on the bottom is "fur." These are the people who lumber around the park in those big animal suits. Last summer Rob was Pluto. Or Goofy. Who can tell them apart? He said it was as hot as blazes in the costume, so I figure Snow White is a good bet because she wears a special outfit, not a big furry suit. Plus I've heard the suits really smell and one kid got lice from sharing the Piglet head.

I pull on the jeans, but as much as I might enjoy being the center of attention, I just can't wear my new leaper shirt to school. Then I open the window, stick my head out, and decide it's too warm for jeans. Five minutes later I'm in the bathroom ironing my hair till it's perfectly straight, while with my free hand I paint my toenails a creamy brown. In between I take bites of my birthday muffin while trying not to spill crumbs on my wet nails. I've always been a very good balancer. I decide on tan cargo pants, chocolate-brown sandals, and a white t-shirt from Express that shows just the right amount of my stomach. When you audition for a role your outfit shouldn't stand out too much. It could distract the director. I learned that from *Entertainment Tonight*.

Rob sticks his head in the bathroom and asks me if I want a ride to school. He usually goes with his friends while I take the school bus with Katy, my best friend since I was three, and Zoey, another one of my close friends who moved next door to Katy when we were in sixth grade. Mom must have put Rob up to it since he never usually offers me a ride.

"No, thanks," I tell him, unable to look up from the job at hand. "You enjoy the last day of the Shark being all yours."

"I really don't mind taking you."

"No, it's okay."

His sigh is audible as he walks away. I'm sure he wishes he didn't have to share the car and I don't blame him. The car has been all his for more than a year. I think he even lost his virginity in it, but that's only a suspicion based on the way his girlfriend, Anne, blushes every time she gets near it. Ever since Rob gained twenty pounds and joined the football team last year as a junior, he went from dweeby smart kid to popular jock and started dating one of the prettiest girls in school. If I gained twenty pounds the guys would go running in the opposite direction. It's so unfair.

I unplug the straightener, swiftly apply the two beauty products I can't live without — mascara and cinnamon-brown lip gloss — and take a last look at the finished product. Hair smooth, skin clear, outfit cool. This is an anomaly for me. It could be weeks until I have a good combo like this again. I have to take advantage of it and make sure I run into Grant Brawner, the senior I've had a crush on since the first day of high school. He designs the playbills for all the school plays, so last fall he had to ask me for a photograph. I told him he could keep it but he said that wouldn't be necessary. I said, no really, he could keep it, and he said, really, he wouldn't need it and gave it back to me as soon as he scanned it in. I like that he's artistic. At least he says "hi" to me when we pass in the halls.

I head downstairs with two minutes to spare before the bus

comes. As usual, the smell of fresh-baked muffins rises to greet me. As for decorations, my parents have really outdone themselves this year. Streamers and balloons line the front hallway. There's even a piñata in the shape of a spaceship hanging from a hook where a plant used to be.

I'm admiring the piñata when my mother comes out of the kitchen. She's wearing the KISS THE COOK apron that I got her last Christmas. I think the reason my mother and I get along so well is that she never really judges me or bosses me around like some of my friends' mothers do to them. She usually doles out her advice in one-liners. For the past few years she's kind of kept her distance, except on my Leap Day birthdays, when it's the opposite. I used to wonder why she backed away, but now I think it's the perfect arrangement. This way we rarely fight about anything.

"Do you like the piñata?" she asks, handing me another muffin-and-candle combo.

"It's great," I tell her. "But aren't I a little old?" I blow out the candle. World peace, baby.

"The man at the party store said candy-filled piñatas are all the rage at parties for four-year-olds. I think he misunderstood me when I said it was only your fourth birthday, and I didn't have the energy to explain it to him. I figured we'd break it open later when your grandparents get here for dinner. Are you sure you don't want to invite any of your friends?"

"I'm sure," I tell her as I stuff the second muffin into my book-bag. "We're going downtown after dinner, so I'll see them then." My family is pretty cool, but the less time mixing friends and family the better.

"Ah, the Sweet Sixteen Initiation at the lake," she says almost wistfully. "I'd forgotten about that."

9

My eyes widen. "You know about that?"

"I was sixteen once too, you know. In this very town." She walks to the curb with me and we wait for the bus together. "I promise I won't ask about what you do tonight if you don't ask what I did all those many years ago."

Even though I know my mom would never ask me about my night, I say, "Deal." We shake on it. "But I don't even know what's supposed to happen. No one will tell me."

"That's the downside of turning sixteen before all your friends," Mom says. "Someone has to go first."

"Can you just give me a hint?"

She laughs and shakes her head. "It's different for everyone."

"It might not even matter, because if I fail my driver's test I'm not going."

"Oh, that reminds me," she says, reaching into her apron pocket. "Here's the note excusing you from third period."

I take the note and slip it into one of the deep pockets of my cargo pants. "Dad's picking me up, right?"

"He'll be there, don't worry. If you're not going to eat that extra muffin you should give it to Megan. The last time she was here for dinner I swear the girl only ate two kernels of corn."

My mother and my friend Megan Panopolis's mother went to high school together, so Mom treats Megan like a second daughter. Actually, she may show a bit more concern for Megan!

"She won't eat it, Mom. I've tried. She's trying out for the part of Belle in *Beauty and the Beast* at Disney-MGM this summer and thinks she has to lose weight." Megan and I have promised never to try out for the same part so we'll never jeopardize our friendship. So far it's working great, and we keep each other motivated.

"She's perfectly fine the way she is," my mother insists. "I'm going to have a talk with her mother."

"I don't think it will help," I say as the bus pulls up.

"Good luck with Juliet!" Mom says as I climb the three steps up. "Break a leg!" She waves goodbye as I take my seat by the window next to Katy. Some people would be embarrassed to have their mother wave to them from the bus stop, but I have a very high embarrassment threshold. It has served me well over the years. Katy practically melts into the ground whenever her mother even talks to her in public. Granted, her mother is pretty strange. Ten years of working as the set designer for the "It's a Small World" ride was bound to cause some permanent damage.

Katy says happy birthday and gives me a big hug. I turn around to look for Zoey, who usually sits right behind Katy. Zoey respects the fact that Katy and I are best friends and leaves the seat next to Katy for me. I would do the same for her and Megan, except Megan doesn't take our bus. Zoey isn't in her seat today.

I turn back around. "Where's Zoey?"

"She called me at six-thirty this morning," Katy explains, stretching her long legs out into the aisle. "She had a self-tanning incident."

"Again?" Zoey is so pale she's not allowed to sit in the sun at all. She and her brother both have light red hair and white skin. It looks good on Zoey. Her brother, Dennis, who is a junior, just looks pasty. Although that may be a side effect of staying in his room all day partying and only listening to Pink Floyd. Their mother has this obsession with skin cancer. You'd think their family would have considered that before moving to Florida. This is the third time this year Zoey has had a mishap with self-tanners. I personally think she does it so she'll look like Megan, who has naturally olive-colored skin. Poor Zoey always turns orange instead of olive.

"She'll be at the lake tonight, though, right?"

Katy nods. "Her mother's making her scrub it all off with this special ammonia stuff, and then she'll drive her to school later."

The best-looking guy in our grade, Jason Count, gets on at the next stop. Since everything is working with my appearance today, I'll be brave and smile at him. The corners of my lips begin turning upright in preparation. Then Jason's girlfriend, Erica or Emily or Emma or some such name that starts with an *E*, steps onto the bus after him.

"She doesn't even live near here," Katy whispers as they take a seat in the back.

"Do you think she spent the night at his house?" I whisper back.

Katy turns her head to look at them. "She's practically sitting in his lap."

I steal a glance at them and they do look very cozy with his strong arms around her. I wonder if I'll ever have a real boyfriend to get cuddly with. Andrew was more of a make-out-behind-the-bleachers kind of guy.

"So did you get the car key yet?" Katy asks.

I dig out my key chain and show it to her. "It's the big shiny one that says Ford on it."

"This is the key chain your leapmate sent you, right? I'm surprised he found one with *Josie* on it. I mean, Pussycats aside, I didn't think it was that popular a name."

"Chris special-ordered them all. He's really sweet."

"Did you ever think of maybe dating him some day? I know he lives on the opposite end of the country, but maybe you could go to the same college or something."

I put the keys back in the side pocket of my bookbag. "I don't think I'm his type."

"Why not?"

"I'm pretty sure he's gay."

She looks surprised. "Why would you think that?"

"Well, for one thing he told me his friends are taking him to a club called The Pink Triangle for his birthday. And once he asked me if it's difficult to get a job singing in the Main Street Parade at Disney."

Katy nods knowingly. "You're probably right, then."

It's a well-known fact at our school that any guy who is either in the Main Street Parade or performs in one of the EPCOT shows is not going to be asking any girls to the prom.

We're still a block away from school when the engine starts sputtering and the bus grinds to a halt. The driver opens the door. "Everybody out."

"Hey," Katy says as we file down the stairs and head toward the school. "At least this time there's no smoke coming out of the back of the bus."

"Soon we'll be in the Shark and won't have to deal with the humiliation of arriving by bus."

"Not soon enough for me," Katy says, pushing open the heavy wooden door at the side entrance of the school.

The halls of the school are covered with bright posters advertising upcoming activities.

COME TRY OUT FOR THE MOST TRAGIC LOVE STORY OF ALL TIME:

SHAKESPEARE'S *ROMEO & JULIET*

SEVENTH PERIOD AND AFTER SCHOOL IN THE AUDITORIUM, FEBRUARY 29

My hands itch to pull it down. The fewer people who know about it, the better. Luckily my better judgment prevails. Katy and

I continue through the throng of rushing students and part ways at the door of my homeroom English class. She pushes a note into my hand.

"You wrote me one already? School hasn't even started yet."

"It's a special birthday note," she says, with an emphasis on the word *special*. "Make sure no one reads it over your shoulder."

"Okay," I stick the note deep in my pocket. "See you in gym."

The bell rings as I slip into my seat. I look up to see HAPPY 4TH BIRTHDAY, JOSIE! on the blackboard. I wonder who wrote it. A bunch of people smile at me as I look around the room, so I can't be sure. Mrs. Greenspan is going through the aisles, handing back last week's homework with the usual bounce in her step. Mrs. G is a great teacher, but she gives more homework than anyone else. She says she does it because she cares. I've yet to figure that one out.

Mitch Hurley probably wrote my birthday message. I know he has a little crush on me because his mother — who is friends with my mother — once found a valentine in his room with my name on it. He never gave me the card, though, so maybe he changed his mind. When Mitch sees me looking at him just now he blushes and then covers his face. Yup, he did it. I think it's kind of funny that anyone would like me. If they only knew what goes on inside my head.

Chapter 1B: Everyone

In her sleep, Josie Taylor tosses and turns on the floor, unaware she has just smacked her forearm against the side of the bed. Two days from now someone in gym class will ask where she got that nasty bruise, and she'll turn her wrist around and be surprised to see it. She is dreaming that the radio has announced that everyone must take cover — a satellite is falling from the sky. She is running across the lawn at school trying to reach the building, but her legs are all rubbery and she can barely make them move. Every once in a while she makes a little noise and almost, but not quite, pulls herself out of her dream.

Rob Taylor has been awake since 5:30, and now that he's finished his hundred sit-ups, he's instant-messaging online with his girlfriend, Anne Derkin. She's also been awake for a long time because she just colored her hair. She's afraid it has a tint of green to it, but since Rob is colorblind she doesn't think he'll notice.

RaggedyAnne13: so you'll pick me up for school?

FootballRobT: yup. i'll be there early. that way we won't have to rush out of the car, if you get my drift . . .

RaggedyAnne13: i'll wear the grape lip balm you like so much

FootballRobT: it's the strawberry one that I like :o)

RaggedyAnne13: i'll wear them both ;-)

FootballRobT: gotta go, it's Josie's birthday today and i have to help the rents decorate the house, hang the pinata, that kind of stuff

RaggedyAnne13: WOW, you guys go all out for a birthday. i'm lucky if i get a card from my family!

FootballRobT: really gotta go, i hear her alarm going off. love you

RaggedyAnne13: see u soon

Rob logs off and stares at the little IM box for a few seconds. *See u soon.* That's the best she could come up with? In all these months that he's been using the L-word, Anne has never said it back. He can hear his parents moving around downstairs and hurries down to join them. Josie's Leap Day birthdays are pretty fun, and they come with free pizza from Domino's. Mom saw to it that Josie was one of the first hundred leapers registered when Domino's started the promotion, and now she gets free pizza for life, each Leap Day birthday.

"Rob," his mother asks as he slides into the kitchen on his socks. "Will you take down the plant in the den and hang this up?" She hands him the spaceship piñata.

Rob shakes it. "Where's the candy?"

"It's not in there? It must have come separately." She rifles through the big bag from Fat Paulie's Party Store and pulls out a plastic container full of assorted candy and chocolates.

Rob opens the top of the spaceship and scoops the candy into it. Tootsie Rolls and tiny boxes of Nerds and packs of Smarties drop inside with pleasing *plunks*. Even though he hasn't even eaten breakfast, he's very tempted to stuff some candy in his mouth. But then Anne's *See u soon* runs through his mind, and he knows that if he gains any more weight he won't be able to turn it into muscle and he'll just get fat. Then it'll be Anne saying, *See u later, I'm finding a new boyfriend.*

"Where'd you stick the balloons?" Josie's father asks as he opens and shuts the two hall closets.

"They're in the trunk of my car," Josie's mother answers, her mouth full of homemade birthday muffin. She decides she used too much salt and smushes some sugar on the top to try and balance it out.

Josie's father lifts the car key off the hook on the kitchen wall and heads out to the garage. A slight chill still hangs in the air and it reminds him of how he used to leave for work every day at this time. He'd head downtown with a hot cup of coffee in one hand and the briefcase his father gave him when he passed the CPA exam twenty years ago in the other. Now the briefcase is in the corner of his home office collecting dust. He reaches into the deep trunk and carefully grasps the strings of sixteen multicolored helium balloons and one silver Mylar one. The approach of Josie's sixteenth birthday made him start thinking about what he had wanted to do with his life back when he was sixteen. He had wanted to help people. But not just people anywhere; he wanted to help people at Disney World. Most people don't think that anyone needs help there, but they do. When he was sixteen he went on a class trip to Disney World, which had just opened a few years before. He had slipped away to find an ice cream cone and stumbled across a little boy crying on a bench in a still undeveloped part of the park. No one else was around.

"Hey mister, do you know where Mickey Mouse is?" the boy had asked, sniffling. "My mama said he was here but I don't see him nowhere."

No one had ever called him "mister" before. "Where's your mother now?"

The boy shrugged and his face started to crumple again.

"Let's go find Mickey," he said, taking the boy's hand. Quietly he asked a girl selling popcorn where he would return a lost child. She directed him to City Hall at the end of Main Street. A "guest relations host" came right over and brought the boy to his frantic mother, then took them to see Mickey Mouse, and then gave the boy a free ice cream cone. Josie's father knows this because he followed them.

From that moment on, he had wanted that man's job. He wanted to be a guest relations host at the Magic Kingdom. In fact, that's why he moved here from Tampa after college. But then he got married and started having kids and there was no way he could pursue his dream. But now the kids are almost out of the house, and he has carefully planned for their college educations. Still, he is dreading telling his family that for the past two weeks he has spent every afternoon training for his new part-time job. They will think he has gone insane. Maybe six months of being out of work will do that to a guy.

He hurries back into the house.

* * *

17

Rob sees the look of determination on his sister's face when he teases her about failing her driver's test. He admires her. On some level she must know she's not the world's greatest driver, but she's determined to pass. She's always been much more willing to take risks and try new things, whereas he would rather blend into the background. It was Josie who brought home the notice about football tryouts last year and stuck it on the fridge so he'd have to see it every time he walked by. He gets the feeling that Josie doesn't know how special she is. When she closes her door to get dressed, he decides he'll offer to drive her to school today and he'll tell her that he's proud of her. It'll be his birthday present to her. He and Anne can be alone later.

Josie's parents finish taping up the streamers so Josie will see them when she comes down for breakfast.

"Honey," Josie's father says tentatively as he ties a yellow balloon around the banister in the front hall, "do you remember what you wanted to do with your life when you were a kid?"

Josie's mom pauses. "I wanted to be a ballerina." Then she laughs. "But my body had other ideas." By the time Josie's mom was twelve, she had the biggest bust and hips in the seventh grade. She is grateful that Josie takes after her father, small and slight, and is spared the teasing she had to endure. She steps into the kitchen and calls out, "Why do you ask?"

He focuses intently on the green streamer in his hand, then replies, "I was just thinking, since I have some time on my hands now, that maybe I'd start a new part-time gig. Something to keep me busy while the recruiter tries to find me a new job." He joins her in the kitchen and holds his breath as he waits for her response.

Taking the rest of the muffins out of the oven, Josie's mom says, "I think that's a great idea. You should definitely do it." She turns and flips open her notebook to make sure she has all the ingredients she needs for the day ahead. Josie's dad waits for her to ask what the new hobby is, but she doesn't. He backs out of the room and goes into his office. While he waits for the computer to boot up he feels a new excitement bubble up in him. Maybe it would be good to tell them about his new plan on Josie's Leap Day birthday. There's just something special about this day. He looks out the window and sees his wife and daughter waiting at the street corner for the bus. He feels blessed that his family members like each other. It was an unexpected gift.

Six blocks away, Jason Count sits on the curb in front of his house. He is stroking his girlfriend Emily Caldwell's back as they wait for the bus. Thank god she decided to come to his house last night instead of running away again. His mother had been very cool about letting her stay in the guest room. She even lent her a t-shirt for school because Emily's tank top didn't cover the bruise on her upper arm. As they wait for the bus Jason fantasizes about punching Emily's father in the face. Jason will never get the chance. Tonight, Mr. Caldwell will leave Bryan's Pub and will ignore the frantic honks of the oncoming motorcycle. He will soar eight feet in the air before breaking his leg in four places. The twenty-five-year-old motorcyclist will be paralyzed from the waist down for the rest of his life. From then on, Emily's father will walk without raising his head so he doesn't have to meet people's eyes. He will never touch another drop of alcohol, or his daughter, again.

Katy Parker looks out the streaky bus window as it approaches her best friend Josie's stop. She closes the poetry notebook that was open on her lap and slips it into her bag. She's been writing poetry since she was eight, but she's never let anyone read it. It is embarrassing to her that she gets straight A's but can't write a poem worth showing anyone.

Katy is excited to give Josie her present tonight at the lake. She and Zoey and Megan chipped in for it. They wanted to get her something unique, not just a bracelet or a gift certificate to the mall. As the bus pulls up Katy thinks that Josie doesn't look near sixteen. They used to be the same height until puberty hit and Katy shot up five inches. Now she feels gangly and awkward next to Josie, like her arms and legs belong to someone else. As Josie climbs on, Katy slips the birthday note she wrote at 1:00 A.M. into the front pocket of her jeans. She had tried telling Josie the contents of the note yesterday because she thought she would burst if she didn't, but she couldn't get up the nerve. She is still undecided about whether she'll give it to her or not. She's not sure how Josie will take the news. And she's not sure if she's ready for the outcome.

Mr. Polansky removes the sign-up list from the wall outside the drama studio. He quickly scans through the list of students who have signed up to audition for his play this afternoon. He is pleased to see some newcomers, along with a few returning students whom he hasn't seen in a few years, and some regulars. He is not surprised to see that Josie Taylor's name is the first one on the list in the Juliet category. She must have signed up the moment he thumbtacked the sheet to the bulletin board. He's never had a student quite like her. Oh sure, he's had determined kids before, but Josie is different. She had wanted the lead role in the fall musical so badly, he felt he couldn't possibly deny her. And she did a perfectly fine job as Anna. It's the air of desperation about it that worries him. Her friend Megan Panopolis has signed up for the audition also, but for the role of Juliet's nurse. With only three female roles of any substance in the play, he's going to have to think long and hard about what to do.

"All right, Mom!" Zoey yells from her bed. She retreated here after calling Katy and hasn't been able to motivate herself out of it again. "Hold your horses. I said I'll wash it off."

"I don't understand why you keep doing this to yourself," her mother responds, leaning her weight against Zoey's door. "You're a lovely girl just the way you are. Your brother doesn't mind being pale."

Zoey thinks it's ridiculous when her mother compares her to Dennis. They couldn't possibly be more different. She doesn't bother to respond. Instead, she throws the patchwork quilt over her head and does what she always does when she's upset. She holds her breath and thinks of things to look forward to. First on her list is the lake tonight and all the new experiences it could provide for her. If Josie doesn't pass her driving test tonight, Zoey knows there will be no party. At this point the test could go either way. And then what will she have to look forward to?

Before Zoey's family moved to Florida, she was so timid that sometimes people would talk to her and she couldn't even answer them. The words would be right on her tongue, but she couldn't get them out. When they moved here it was a fresh start. She decided that she would be a new person. A person who had friends. Who had *fun*. And it worked! Katy came over from next door the day Zoey's family arrived in Orlando, and then she introduced Zoey to Megan and Josie the next week. She was instantly drawn to Megan, who seemed so exotic and who made every occasion fun without even trying. Sometimes, in the dark moments of the night, Zoey fears that without her new friends, she might revert back to her old self and blend into the woodwork again. If Zoey doesn't have every experience offered to her now, she's afraid her time will run out. Her mother knocks on the door and tells her to get in the shower, but Zoey pretends not to hear and burrows deeper into the sheets.

Mrs. Joy Greenspan checks the clock over the door and sees she still has time before the bell rings. Sometimes she thinks the homeroom bell is the best sound in the world. She knows she should be burned out by now, after twenty-five years of teaching, but she still loves it. Everyone says her first name fits her to a tee. Joy. She hated the name when she was younger but now it pleases her. She goes to the window and pours out the dregs of her third cup of coffee before heading to the blackboard to write, HAPPY 4TH BIRTHDAY, JOSIE! She wipes the excess chalk dust off on her skirt, glad to have remembered her student's special birthday. Reading the students' files each August has served her well. She knows who is on Ritalin, who has the highest IQ, who the lowest, and who once started

These are the things I'm afraid of: an airplane falling on my house, the dark, being in small places, failing my driver's test, spiders, drowning, snakes, never growing taller, never getting out of this town, alligators, war, anyone in my family dying, having my friends turn against me, eels, getting old, ghosts (including the ones that get in your car at the Haunted Mansion), letting everyone down, and never falling in love. Oh, and I'm also petrified of tornadoes. We get them sometimes here in central Florida and it scares me to death. When my mother was growing up on the outskirts of town, her younger brother was plucked from his very own bed as if the hand of God came down and took him. He was found on the front porch with nearly every bone in his body broken. He didn't make it through the night. My mother said that next to his body was a whole pile of fish — even though they didn't live anywhere near a lake — and some smashed tomatoes, which aren't even native to Florida. Now I'm older than my own uncle ever got to be. It's weird.

But on the positive side, I'm not afraid of heights, clowns, or public speaking. The only day of the year when I'm not afraid of dying is my birthday. I mean, the odds of both being born *and* dying on Leap Day are practically astronomical. Sometimes when I get up in the morning I wonder if I'll die before I get back in my bed. Today I breathe a little easier. I know I will sleep in my bed tonight. Or at worst, on my floor.

I wish Katy hadn't given me her note until after first period. Besides Mrs. Greenspan's love of homework, she has a nasty habit of confiscating notes and posting them on the bulletin board. I decide not to even take it out of my pocket so I'm not tempted to read it.

Last month Katy and I were on this kick where we'd exchange notes with dirty limericks about *The Brady Bunch*. It's a good thing no one saw those. They'd have us committed. Katy is a pretty good poet, though. I think she has a future in it.

Jeff Grand runs in just as the late bell rings and I hand him last night's physics homework as he passes my desk. He takes it without a word. It's an unspoken understanding that he didn't do the assignment and will need to copy mine. I don't mind. I feel I owe him something. When we were all eight years old, me, him, Megan, and Katy played doctor once, but the three of us refused to show him ours after he had been so gracious as to show us his. We ran back through the woods while he stood there with a red face hurrying to button up his shorts. To this day I can still picture those green-and-blue-striped shorts. Anyway, he's taking a chance copying from me because I'm what is known as the Typical "B" Student. Do my homework, but not extra credit. Study for tests, but not a second longer than I have to. Every report card says the same thing, "Josie could get A's if she applied herself." Let Rob be the smart one in the family. I don't even think I want to go to college. I'd rather go to acting school. The one class I get A's in is drama.

Mrs. G takes attendance differently than any other teacher. "Jared Adams?" she asks, knowing very well he's sitting right there in the first seat.

"Ubiquitous," Jared responds. "Existing everywhere at the same time."

"Very good, sweetie," she replies. "Tara Bantok?"

Tara pauses for a second and then says, "Reciprocate. A mutual or equivalent exchange or a paying back of what one has received."

It goes on like this, all around the room. Every Monday we have to respond with a different SAT word and definition from this huge list Mrs. G gave us in the beginning of the year. If she especially likes your word, she'll call you sweetie or baby or honey. Mrs. G must be in her fifties but is very perky and energetic. The way she bounces around the room reminds me of Tigger from Winnie-the-Pooh. When she calls out Zoey's name I debate telling Mrs. G why Zoey's not here, but what would I say? Zoey turned orange today and will be late?

"Josie Taylor?"

I completely forgot the word I had chosen for today. I wrack my brain and think of a word from the theater. "Um, soliloquy? A dramatic monologue that gives the illusion of being a series of unspoken reflections."

"Excellent, baby," she says, beaming. She then turns to the blackboard and gestures with her attendance book. "So today's your birthday, Josie. Can you explain to us why it's only your fourth?"

Most of the kids already know since they've known me since kindergarten, but who am I to turn down an opportunity to have everyone pay attention to me? A mini-performance. "Do you want me to go up front, or just stay here?"

"From your seat is fine."

"Okay," I say, slightly disappointed. "Well, February twenty-ninth only comes around once every four years, when there's a leap year. So this is only the fourth time in my life that I've actually had a birthday."

"And why do we have leap year?" Mrs. Greenspan prompts me.

This answer I know like the back of my hand. "Because it really takes the earth three hundred sixty-five *and a quarter* days to go around the sun, so we make up for the quarter day by adding a full day every four years. Otherwise, the seasons would get all messed up and eventually Christmas would wind up in the summer."

"So what's wrong with that?" Missy Hiver calls out. "I think that would be cool!"

I really do not like Missy Hiver. She's been trying to compete with me since the second grade, when she told our teacher that she should be the carrot in the school vegetable parade instead of me because I was too short. She also has this weird obsession with Mary-Kate and Ashley Olsen, those twins who have their own television shows, movies, clothing and makeup lines, CDs, books, and private jet. In eighth grade she was Mary-Kate for Halloween in the morning and then Ashley in the afternoon. As much as I can't stand her, I have to admit that was pretty clever.

"You might want to reconsider that, Missy," Mrs. G says. "You already have summers off from school, so you wouldn't get an additional Christmas vacation."

That shuts her up fast. After Mrs. G finishes taking attendance, she erases my happy birthday greeting and writes, CONTEMPLATING YOUR NAVEL. "Now, what does this mean?" she asks.

A hand shoots up from the back. "Does it have something to do with deciding whether or not to get a bellybutton piercing?"

Mrs. Greenspan smiles thinly. "No, it doesn't."

Amelia Peters tentatively raises her hand. Amelia pretends to be shy and quiet in front of the teachers, but she's really the opposite. She wears a big cross around her neck and her parents make her wear a uniform every day like she goes to Catholic school instead of public. I steer clear of her whenever I can. Since Amelia so rarely volunteers, Mrs. Greenspan immediately acknowledges her. Amelia lets her arm fall slowly as she asks, "Is contemplating your navel the question of whether Adam and Eve had bellybuttons if they were not born of man?"

"Not exactly," Mrs. Greenspan says with a sigh. She turns back to the class. "It's simply an expression of deep thought and introspection in the absence of other activity. I had hoped some of you might be able to connect it to *Walden Pond,* which we've been reading for the past two weeks."

"I was going to say that," Missy Hiver mutters loud enough for everyone to hear, "but I thought it was too obvious."

Mrs. Greenspan flashes her a wan smile and then says, "On Wednesday we will begin *The Scarlet Letter,* and in preparation, I'm going to ask you all to be introspective. Since the book is about judging right and wrong, let's talk about the seven deadly sins for a minute. Then later in the week we'll discuss how they are portrayed in literature. Can anyone list them?"

No one answers. Amelia slowly raises her hand again and in almost a whisper rattles off, "Pride, envy, gluttony, lust, anger, greed, and sloth." Then she sinks a little into her chair.

"That's right, honey," Mrs. G says after a short pause. "Very good." As soon as Mrs. G turns around to write them on the board, Amelia smirks. I copy the list into my notebook, titling it THE SEVEN DEADLIES.

"Now I want all of you to pay attention over the next week, to each time one of these emotions enters your life. I'm hoping this will help you identify with Hester Prynne, Hawthorne's main character."

What kind of name is Hester Prynne? Thank god the bell rings before I have to find out. Mitch Hurley passes my desk on the way to the door and I want to thank him for the birthday wishes, but he just ducks his head and speeds up. Jeff Grand drops my physics homework on my desk. I'm about to slip it into my notebook when I notice the blue Post-it note he stuck on top. I read it as I head out into the crowded hallway. It says, "Do you think Katy would go to the prom with me if I asked?" When I look up from the note Jeff is nowhere in sight. I don't know how to break it to him, but sophomores don't get to go to the prom unless they're asked by a junior or senior. That boy is really out of the loop. All we have is a dorky spring dance called, imaginatively enough, the Spring Dance. I guess this means Jeff's forgiven Katy for leaving him with his pants down. I feel a little pang of something that's not really jealousy, because I'm not interested in Jeff in that way, but still. A little pang that no one wants to ask me to the prom. And there's only sixty-five days left, if you don't count weekends.

We barely have five minutes between classes, a schedule no doubt intended to limit the amount of trouble we can get ourselves into in the hallways. My photography class is on the other side of the building and I debate my two current options. Option A: Go to the bathroom. Option B: Take the route that will intersect with Grant Brawner as he heads to his next class on the second floor. Even though he didn't want to keep my picture, I'm not ready to give up on him. Bathroom, Grant. Grant, bathroom. My bladder says bathroom, but my heart says Grant. Plus, soon my hair will start to unstraighten, and I don't want to lose the birthday glow. I tear down the hall and up the stairs. If I'm off by even a minute, our paths won't cross. When I reach the second floor I'm about to admit defeat until I spy the back of his head about ten people in front of me. I race up ahead of him, on the other side of the crowd, and then turn around as though I had been walking in that direction from the beginning. Now he's heading right toward me as planned. I try to act casual and glance at yet another poster advertising today's audition. At the exact right second, I lift my arm to wave hello. But just before his eyes land on me, someone grabs my arm and pulls me to the side of the hall. I look up to find Katy.

"What are you doing?" I ask, not bothering to keep the frustration out of my voice. "I was about to run into Grant." I watch as he walks into his classroom, unaware of all my efforts.

"I'm sorry," Katy says, not sounding sorry enough if you ask me. "Look, do you still have that note I gave you before homeroom?"

"Yeah, why?"

"Can I have it back?"

"But I didn't read it yet."

"That's okay," she says. "I'll give it back later. I, uh, I just want to add something."

"A *Brady Bunch* limerick?"

She pauses. "Sure, yeah, a *Brady Bunch* limerick."

I look at my watch. The bell is going to ring any second. I dig into the deep pocket of my pants and pull out the note. Katy grabs it and turns to go with a breathless, "Thanks." She ducks into her history class across the hall just as the bell rings. Meanwhile, I'm still on the other end of school from where I need to be.

Crap.

Chapter 2B: Everyone

The halls are thinning out, and Jeff Grand knows he's barely going to make it to homeroom before the late bell rings. He hates that he'll have to ask Josie Taylor for her physics homework again. Not because he doesn't like her, but because he knows she thinks he must be stupid. And he's not stupid. It's just that both of his parents work full time and he has a lot of responsibilities. For the past three years, his parents have been in charge of the primate section of Disney's Animal Kingdom. By the time they come home at seven, they smell like monkey poop and his mother barely has enough energy to cook dinner. This means that more often than not, Jeff has to take care of his four-year-old sister, Sage, do the laundry and the grocery shopping, and fix whatever appliance needs fixing. His only solace is watching reruns of *The Simpsons* each night at 11:00. There's simply no time to do his own homework. He just cannot do everything.

As Jeff approaches Josie's desk, she already has the homework assignment in her hand. She passes it off to him like the seasoned pro she is. He wants to say thank you, but Mrs. G is already starting attendance and he doesn't want to draw her attention. By the time he sits down, Tara has just said the word *reciprocate* and it makes him think that he should reciprocate for Josie's help somehow. He should do something nice for her.

As soon as Tara says *reciprocate* she files it into the back of her brain without even realizing it. Mrs. G goes on to the next person, and Tara takes out a blue nail file from her pencil case. With her hands under her desk, she files off the sharp edge of her right pinky nail that had been bothering her since breakfast. Tara is what her mother likes to call *pleasantly plump* but Tara prefers the term *chubby*. Instead of feeling sorry for herself, she considers herself lucky. She assumes that none of the boys are interested in her, so she focuses her energy on her schoolwork and gets all A's and B-pluses in high-level classes without worrying about competing with the skinny girls for the cutest guys. She is also fond of her nails. They are very long and she paints each one a different pastel shade.

Tara watches as Josie Taylor stands up at her desk and pushes her long hair behind her ears. Tara wonders how Josie gets her hair to be so straight. Last week it was kind of frizzy — not very frizzy, but sort of bushy — and then today it is smooth as silk. Tara would hate it if her birthday only came around once every four years. But Josie seems to like it for some reason. Tara looks over at Missy Hiver, who rolls her eyes. Tara doesn't know why Missy doesn't like Josie, but everyone knows she doesn't. In seventh grade Tara saw Missy steal Josie's math homework at lunch and slip it into the trash so when Josie went to look for it later it wasn't there.

Missy Hiver only half-listens to what Josie is blabbing on about. When she sees an opening to cut in, she does, even though she really *doesn't* think it would be cool if Christmas came in the summer. Once it's out of her mouth she wishes she hadn't said anything. She glares at the back of Josie's head and is filled with a familiar feeling in the pit of her stomach. When Missy was born, she had a twin who died within the day because her lungs were filled with fluid. Her parents had named her Jocelyn, and her mom said they would have called her Josie for short. Missy mourns the loss of this twin, this missing half of herself, every day. She hates that Josie Taylor is here instead of *her* Josie. It just screams unfairness and mocks her every time she has to hear Josie's name being called. She and Josie even look sort of alike. They both have long hair, but Missy has a larger nose and Josie has a small mouth that reminds Missy of a fish. For a brief second in art class last year Missy considered sneaking up behind Josie and cutting off her hair with one swift snip of the scissors. She actually had to sit on her hands until the urge passed. She cried herself to sleep that night without even realizing it.

Missy knows people think she is very immature to be obsessed with

Mary-Kate and Ashley at her age, when most girls outgrow them by the time they are twelve. But she also knows that Mary-Kate would understand her pain if she had to be without Ashley. They are never apart. They do all the same things she and Josie (*her* Josie) would do. They shop together and work together and study together and go on double dates. They are BEST friends. Missy listens to that pretend goody-two-shoes, holier-than-thou Amelia Peters recite the seven deadly sins and almost laughs when she hears the word *envy*. Missy envies everybody. But especially Mary-Kate and Ashley. Plus, no one wrote happy birthday to *her* on the blackboard when *she* turned sixteen last month.

Amelia Peters swears she can feel the gold cross around her neck burning her flesh. How well she knows those seven deadly sins. Her parents have been reminding her of them since the day she was born. When she was younger she tried to be so good, so pure and righteous. Everyone else is copying down the list so they can record each time they commit one of them. Amelia doesn't need to. She can think of twenty times off the top of her head that she's committed these sins. In fact, she tries to commit each sin at least once a day. Her favorites are lust and gluttony. They work well together. Anger is a waste of energy, so she saves that for when she sees some sort of injustice in the world. Which, in high school, usually happens by lunchtime.

Jeff Grand figures out how he can do a favor for Josie to show his appreciation. He can ask Josie's friend Katy to the prom! He figures Josie has a date already, but Katy probably doesn't because she seems to hang in Josie's shadow. With a best friend like Josie, who is kind of shiny and glowy and has a brother on the football team, Katy must feel like second fiddle. If he asked her to the prom, then she'd feel more special and Josie wouldn't have to feel guilty about hogging the spotlight all the time. Excited about the cleverness of his plan, Jeff sticks a Post-it note on Josie's homework before handing it back to her at the end of class.

Mitch Hurley watches Josie as she stands in the hallway reading a Post-it note with a strange expression on her face. She pauses like she's deep in thought and then suddenly takes off down the hall at full speed, almost knocking him to the floor. He watches her go and wishes he had the nerve to talk to her. He wishes he had given her that Valentine's Day card in eighth grade, but after his mother saw it he threw it out and now he's not sure why. He's seen every play Josie's been in since grammar school, even the show where she played some kind of round vegetable. She still smiled valiantly like a true professional. Last fall he saw *The King and I* three times. It was about time she got the lead role. He doesn't think he's obsessed or anything, he just knows a quality person when he sees one. He feels that he is an excellent judge of character and can size up a person's motivations in under a minute. He thought he was going to pass out when Josie looked at him in class before. He couldn't imagine why she was looking at him, and she was even smiling. He had immediately covered his nose, sure that he had something hanging out of it because that would be just his luck.

On the other end of the school, Katy Parker is running through the halls, totally freaking out. All she can think about is getting that note back from Josie. She didn't hear a word her French teacher said all period. She's pretty sure Josie wouldn't have tried to read the note in Mrs. Greenspan's class, so as long as she can catch her before her next class she should be okay. She runs up to the photography lab but Josie hasn't gotten there yet. She waits at the door, scanning down the hall in both directions. If she doesn't leave now, she'll be late for her American History class, and there's a test today. Reluctantly, she heads in the direction of class and prays she'll run into Josie on the way.

A few steps ahead of Katy, Grant Brawner is walking to his next class with his friend Stu.

"Just cut with me, Grant. Don't be such a loser."

"Are you trying to peer-pressure me?" Grant asks.

Stu grins. "Is it working?"

"Nope. I'm not cutting class and that's final."

"Wuss."

"Delinquent."

Stu pushes Grant into the row of lockers, and they laugh the kind of laugh that only guys who have been friends since first grade can. Grant opens his locker and throws his calculus book inside, and they continue walking.

"Hey," Stu whispers, jabbing Grant in the side. "Here comes that girl who follows you everywhere."

Grant ignores Stu and keeps looking straight ahead.

"She's so determined, dude. And she's kind of cute, even though she comes up to, like, your hip!"

"Shut up," Grant tells him. He's about to say hi to Josie, but Josie's friend comes out of nowhere and pulls her away. Stu laughs and pushes Grant into their classroom.

After accosting Josie in the hall, Katy sits down in her seat in American History and waits for her heart to stop pounding. She is very relieved that the note is safely clenched in her fist. She just didn't feel ready to deal with Josie's reaction to its contents. She opens her hand and lets the balled-up note roll onto the desk. Then her eyes open wide. She hurriedly opens the folded piece of paper and silently reads,

Dear Whomever It May Concern,

Please excuse Josie Taylor from school today at 10:45. She will be taking her driver's exam and will return as soon as it's over.

Sincerely,

Mrs. Laura Taylor

Oh my god! This is the wrong note! If she has this one, that means Josie will have handed *her* note to the office.

Katy jumps out of her seat and runs up to Mr. Maron, her history teacher. "I have to go somewhere," she tells him, trying to keep the panic out of her voice. "It'll just take a minute."

"The test is about to start. You know the rules. No one leaves until the last person hands in his or her paper."

"But I —"

"No buts."

"But —"

"Sit."

Katy debates making a mad dash from the room but knows she could never do it. She returns to her seat and taps her foot incessantly instead.

"Stop," demands the too-much-power-for-his-own-good hall monitor. I screech to a halt only five doors down from the photography lab.

"Do you have a hall pass?" he asks, holding out his hand palm-up. He's actually wearing a sash across his body like he's running for Miss America. Except, instead of Miss Florida, his sash says: OFFICIAL HALL MONITOR, 2ND FLOOR. I've seen him before. He's only a freshman. He should fear me.

"I'm late for class," I tell him. I have to pause to take a breath between *late* and *for.* I really need to start working harder in gym. "It's just right over there." I point. He doesn't even turn to look.

"Why are you late?" he asks, which of course is only making me later.

I can't very well say I was stalking Grant Brawner or that Katy just cornered me, so I stand there staring at him. He takes out his little pad and ever so slowly writes me a detention note.

I can't believe this kid. "Are you serious?"

"Very serious. No one in the halls without a pass. You know the rules."

I consider pulling the old "but I just got my period and I have to run to the bathroom" excuse, but I don't have the nerve. So instead I say, "But it's my birthday!"

"Here you go," he says, handing me the slip. "Don't forget to bring it to the office to schedule your detention. Oh, and happy birthday."

With those words, evil Official Hall Monitor, 2nd Floor walks away. No, *saunters* away. Well, that sucked and now I'm really, really late. I need to plan my entrance carefully. Okay. The door is open, which means no one's in the darkroom yet. I sneak closer to the door and can hear Mr. Simon talking. Maybe he'll be writing something on the board and I can grab one of the stools in the back of the lab. I peek into the room just as Mr. Simon appears directly in front of me. He's even cuter up close. Did I mention how cute he is? All the girls — including me — have crushes on him. He looks like a younger version of Tom Cruise.

"Why, Ms. Taylor. I almost closed the door on you."

I slink past him into the room. "Sorry," I say in a small voice. "I had a run-in with a power-hungry hall monitor." I love how he calls me Ms. Taylor.

He closes the door. "Well class, does anyone think I should reprimand Ms. Taylor for being late on her birthday?"

A chorus of "no's" rises up from the room.

"Guess you're off the hook," he says and starts handing out the strips of negatives that we developed last week. I had told him about my Leap Day birthday a few months ago, but I didn't think he would remember. He's been a little out of it ever since Christmas break, when he married Ms. Robinson, the biology teacher who none of the girls like now. Personally, I think he should have waited seven years and married me, but he didn't ask my opinion. Ms. Robinson seems so cold and uptight and Mr. Simon's so . . . so . . . not those things. He used to have a ponytail but she made him cut it off. As my mom once said, there's no accounting for attraction, although she was referring to the huge sheepdog down the street who trails longingly after Mrs. Mulvaney's old poodle.

A list of other memorable Mom-isms:

1. It's just as easy to love a rich man as a poor man. (Summer of sixth grade when I told her I had a huge crush on a boy in camp who wore the same shorts every day.)

2. The road to hell is paved with good intentions. (This was when I planned on calling my grandparents on their fiftieth anniversary but forgot because *Clueless* was on TV and I love that movie.)

3. An ounce of prevention is worth a pound of cure. (When she made me swallow a mixture of echinacea, zinc, and ground-up vitamin C when the flu was going around.)

4. You'll thank me later. (Following anything that I didn't want to do/buy/say/wear that she makes me do/buy/say/wear anyway.)

5. Why have hamburger when you can have steak? (In response to discussion about teenagers having sex or waiting until they are older and preferably married. I didn't mention that I like hamburgers better than steak, because I didn't think that was the point.)

6. Beauty comes from within. (The day of my eighth-grade yearbook picture when I had a pimple on my cheek the size of Space Mountain.)

Only six people can use the darkroom at once, and unfortunately Mr. Simon calls my group first. Even though photography is my second-favorite class, I was hoping to practice for the audition. One can never ask "Wherefore art thou Romeo?" too many times. I grab my negatives and follow the others into the small room. If the darkroom were any darker, I'd be afraid, but I love its soft reddish glow. I even love all the trays and tongs and the sweet, slightly acrid smell of mysterious chemicals. The whole thing seems romantic and full of creative potential. Like things are being born in here. The lab and the darkroom are very high tech. The whole room was donated by a rich man whose son had graduated from here and had just started his career as a photojournalist when he was killed in the Balkans. It's called the Hunter Koenig Jr. Room. Poor Hunter Jr.

"I cannot work without gloves," Becky Dickson exclaims. "And the box is empty."

"That's why we saved the gloves from last week," Mr. Simon says, reaching under the counter and pulling out a box filled with the yellow gloves.

"I can't wear those! Anyone could have had their hands in there. Do you know how unsanitary that is?"

The rest of us try not to laugh. Becky takes her hygiene very seriously. Laughing only urges her on. The last time we laughed at her she'd told us that every time you flush the toilet, germs fly across the room and land on your toothbrush. Ever since then I can't brush my teeth without thinking of her. She and I used to play together when we were little, but we drifted apart. The only reason I can think of is that Katy and I started getting to be better friends around that time. Maybe Becky got jealous and didn't want to hang out with us.

Mr. Simon appears stumped. "I guess you could wrap your hands in paper towels. That'll offer some protection."

"Fine," she says, and proceeds to do just that. Now she looks like Minnie Mouse, with skinny arms and big puffy hands. "And what about the fumes?" she says, wrapping tape around her hands to keep the "gloves" in place. "You told us the air filter would be fixed over the weekend."

I can tell Mr. Simon is getting irritated. "We haven't even opened the chemicals yet."

"C'mon, Becky," Greg Adler says. "Can you give it a rest? Some of us want to actually start the class." Greg and Becky always make this big show of hating each other, but personally I think they have the hots for each other.

Becky glares at him in the inky darkness. "You only want to hurry up so you can go practice your half Torah like the other thirteen-year-olds."

"It's a *Haf* Torah," Greg growls. "And it's not my fault I had mono when I was thirteen!"

"Maybe it *was* your fault," she says.

"Enough," Mr. Simon says. "I swear you two are worse than an old married couple."

That shuts them up fast and we finally get started. I feed my negative strip under the enlarging machine and slide it through until I find the picture I want to make. I took this particular shot outside at the picnic tables at lunch last week. Zoey is holding up a hot dog and Katy is laughing. Zoey's in the shade and Katy's in the sun, so it's a good study in contrast, which is what the assignment was about. Greg peers over my shoulder.

"Interesting picture, Josie," he says with a little smile on his face. "They look very excited about that hot dog."

"I guess they were hungry," I tell him, adjusting the machine so the picture will be as big as possible. "I think the lighting came out really well."

"Right. The lighting."

I look up at him. "What's that supposed to mean?" I know everyone else is listening but there's nothing I can do about it. Luckily one of the Davis twins — either Tom or Tyson, I can never tell which one especially since they are in all the same classes — freaks out because his negative is blank and everyone rushes over to comfort him. They are sensitive boys. In fifth grade Tom (or maybe

Tyson) cried when our class tadpoles got washed down the sink by mistake. "They'll never be frogs now," he had wailed. Our fifth grade yearbook was later titled *Now We Are Frogs*.

"It doesn't mean anything," Greg says. He glances in Mr. Simon's direction. "Just forget it."

I'm about to insist that he tell me when I remember that Greg played Seven Minutes in the Closet with Zoey at a party the first summer after she moved here. He must like the picture because Zoey's in it. "Don't worry, I won't tell Zoey you ogled her."

"That's not it, Josie," Greg says between gritted teeth. "Can we please just forget it?"

I shrug and use the tongs to lay the piece of photo paper into the first pan.

"Ten more minutes," Mr. Simon announces. I move my picture carefully from pan to pan and then use the rubber clips to hang it from the overhead rope. I hope it will be dry by the end of class so I can show it to Zoey and Katy at lunch.

We file back into the bright light of the lab and the next shift goes in. Mr. Simon asks Greg if he can monitor things in the darkroom because he has to run out for five minutes.

"But Mr. Simon," Greg pleads. "I have to practice."

Mr. Simon groans, picks someone else, and dashes from the room. Greg pushes a stool into the far corner and digs out some folded papers from his bookbag. He spreads them out over his knees and begins chanting quietly in Hebrew. It's very soothing, actually. A Davis twin comes over and sits next to me.

"So it's your birthday?"

"Uh-huh."

"Cool."

"Yeah."

Silence. Then, "Are you getting your license today?"

"Oh, no!" I jump to my feet. "I forgot!"

"You forgot to get your *license?*"

"No, I forgot to hand in my absence note this morning." I pat my pocket and feel the bulge of the note. At least I didn't lose it.

"It's not a big deal. Just hand it in now. Mrs. Lombardo is cool, she won't mind."

"Yeah, but I can't leave until Mr. Simon gets back." I guess teachers need to use the bathroom, too, sometimes. It is turning into a long bathroom trip though. Normally I'd take this time to write a note to Katy, but after she so strangely took hers back I decide not to. Finally, Mr. Simon runs back in and apologizes for being gone so long. I go up to the front of the room and tell him the situation. He tells me to take my stuff with me so I can go straight to my next class since there isn't that much time left before the bell. Mr. Simon is the best.

I'm about to head out of the room when I remember to get a hall pass. That kid isn't going to get me twice! I debate a bathroom stop since now I have the time, but decide I'd better just hand in the note. I stand in front of Mrs. Lombardo's desk waiting for her to look up from her paperwork. She has been at our school since it opened forty years ago. As the main office secretary, nothing gets by her. But since she refuses to use a computer, the stacks of paper on her desk are literally several feet high. She may not even be able to see me. I clear my throat and she looks up, surprised.

"Oh, hello Josie," she says in her too-many-cigarettes-over-too-many-years rasp. "What brings you to my part of town?"

I reach in my pocket and hand the piece of paper across the desk, careful not to knock anything over. She tosses it on the top of the closest pile and says, "Let me guess, it's your birthday and you need to go take your driver's test."

I smile. "You're good."

She shrugs. "It's a gift. Also the mixture of fear and excitement on your face gave me a clue."

I laugh. People always tell me they can tell by my face what I'm thinking. I guess that's what makes me a good actress.

"Good luck on your driver's test," Mrs. Lombardo says, turning her attention back to her work. "You'll do fine."

"Thanks, I hope you're right." I turn to go and remember the detention slip. Grudgingly I dig it out of my back pocket and hand it across the desk. "I forgot to give you this too."

She takes the slip from my hand, looks at it, crumples it up and winks.

I love Mrs. Lombardo. Hurrying from the room before she can change her mind, I realize I still have time to get to the bathroom. As I push open the metal door to the stall I wonder if everyone has a favorite stall or just me. Each bathroom is different. In this one, it's the last stall. But down at the other end of the hall, it's the middle stall. And upstairs it's the last stall again. Sometimes I'll actually leave the bathroom if someone is in my stall. I'm about to flush the toilet when two girls come into the bathroom and immediately start screaming at each other. I sit there and listen, moving my feet back as far toward the toilet as I can.

"You are such a liar," one of them says. "You totally knew we were seeing each other."

"Hooking up one night after a party at the lake is *not* seeing each other."

They are silent for a moment but I can feel the tension through the door. I don't recognize the voices.

"It was more than that one time," the first girl says, her voice bordering on hysterical now.

"Listen, Marissa, I'm sorry, okay? What else do you want me to say? I can't take back what happened, believe me, I wish I could."

"What's that supposed to mean?"

"I mean I wish I hadn't slept with him, it was *so* not worth this."

"You SLEPT with him?" Now the girl is really wailing. "I just thought you fooled around!"

"Why aren't you mad at Steve? He was there too, you know!"

"Because you're supposed to be my friend. He's just a guy." I can hear her pulling the paper towels off the rack. Now she is blowing her nose.

Even though I'm completely riveted, I also wish the bell would ring soon. The walls are starting to close in on me. In a minute I'm going to start sweating. Luckily I don't have much longer to wait. The bell rings, and the front door to the bathroom clicks shut. It's finally quiet. I flush the toilet and walk out of the stall right smack into the crying girl. She seems just as surprised to see me as I am to see her. I recognize her now. Marissa Badish, a senior. She and Rob did a science project together last year.

"Are you gonna be okay?" I ask, running cold water over my hands.

She shakes her head. More people file into the bathroom, but she doesn't budge. "You wouldn't happen to have a cigarette, would you?"

"No." I wish there was something I could do for her. "Do you want me to go find you one?"

A tiny smile flits across her face. "No, that's okay. I'm trying to quit anyway."

"That guy sounds like a jerk," I say, simply because I can't think of anything else. "You're better off without him."

"Probably," she says. "But I really love him." She splashes some water on her face, smoothes her hair, shrugs, then leaves. I stand there for a minute dwelling on her words. Feeling suddenly very immature in comparison to someone who is in love, I consider soaking my crumpled paper towel and throwing it onto the ceiling like we used to in middle school. Luckily, my better judgment prevails, and I toss it into the overflowing garbage and hurry to the gym. I'm not even going to bother getting changed because I'll only be here for twenty minutes before my dad comes. I drop my bookbag on a locker room bench and wonder if Rob loves Anne. If he does, he sure hasn't told me. I can't even imagine what it must feel like to love someone and have them cheat on you.

The other girls start changing into their gym clothes. As usual, Alyssa Levy strolls the full length of the locker room in only her gym shorts. Everyone else changes as quickly as possible, facing the lockers. But not her. She'll even have a conversation with you while she just stands there with her perfectly proportioned breasts held proudly in front of her like they are on display at the science fair. I glance down at my own chest. My birthday wish apparently has not kicked in yet. I decide to wait in the gym. I'm about to push open the swinging door when Katy comes barreling in and grabs me, for the second time in an hour.

"Josie! Did you go down to the office yet?"

"What? Yes, to hand in my absence note. Why?"

"Did you read it first?"

"No, why would I? I gave it to Mrs. Lombardo. It was actually pretty funny."

Katy looks stricken. "Why was it funny?"

"Just that Mrs. Lombardo guessed I was going for my test today, that's all. She didn't even open the note."

Arnold Slotnik whistles as he walks down the hall away from Josie Taylor. It felt as good as he imagined it would to give her that detention slip. If it had been almost anyone else he probably would have let them go. He wishes he could share the experience with his next-door neighbor Mitch Hurley, but Mitch is the last person he can tell. Arnold and Mitch used to play after school for as long as Arnold can remember. They would put on Mitch's dad's old Meatloaf albums and jump around his basement like they were in the band. They played video games for hours until Arnold's mother warned them their eyes would start to bleed if they didn't give it a rest. Then came that fateful day last summer when Arnold opened Mitch's closet by mistake. Sure, it did have NO ADMITTANCE, PRIVATE, and KEEP OUT! THIS MEANS YOU written all over it, but he didn't think Mitch would mind. After all, they were best friends. He was trying to find Mitch's old pair of Rollerblades. Instead he saw all these pictures of the same girl tacked up on the inside of the door. They were mostly cutouts from school playbills; some were class pictures, one or two were from newspapers. He looked closer. One of the photo captions identified the girl as Josie Taylor. He was so stunned at this display that he couldn't tear his eyes away. He was still staring at it when Mitch came in, found him, and told him to leave his house and never come back. Arnold is still furious that Mitch would let a girl come between them. When Arnold is a junior he will develop a huge crush on a girl in his after-school karate class and will steal the top of her uniform so that he can smell her perfume at night. He will finally understand what Mitch was going through.

Arnold stops whistling as he nears the tired-looking man in the crumpled brown suit who is making one of his monthly visits. Arnold no longer bothers to ask the man if he has permission to be here. As they pass in the hall they nod at each other. The man stops next to the closed door of the photography classroom. With a shaky finger he traces the engraved words on the gold plaque to the left of the doorway. As usual, he wonders what his son would think of this gift of his. He has no idea if he would feel pleased, honored, or embarrassed. He comes by here every few weeks just to see Hunter Jr.'s name. It makes him feel good to know that so many children see the plaque each day. Even if they don't give it a second thought. It helps to know that his son is remembered.

"All right, Mom!" Zoey yells from the shower. "I'm almost done!" She adds more of the special ammonia mixture to the loofah and continues to scrub her left arm frantically. Then she holds both arms out next to each other to compare. The left one still looks faintly orange. She continues scrubbing. Her mother knocks again.

"I'm on my last arm," she calls out, scrubbing even harder. She wonders if the ammonia is doing more damage than the fake tan did.

"Can't you just wear a long-sleeved shirt?" her mother asks through the door.

"It's eighty degrees out!"

"You should have thought of that before you got yourself into this mess."

Zoey tries to keep her voice under control. "If you let me sit in the sun every once in a while, I wouldn't have to do this!"

"Do you need me to show you those skin cancer pictures again? Two more minutes and then we absolutely have to get going."

Zoey turns off the water and reaches for the towel. She catches her reflection in the mirror over the sink. Her face still has a slight orange tinge to it, contrasting horribly with her red hair. That guy from Orlando South High promised to come to Josie's party tonight. She really wanted to look good for him. Too late for that. She calls out, "What if I just don't go to school today at all?" She holds her breath and waits for her mother's reply.

"That's fine," her mother says, and Zoey feels a surge of happiness. "But then you're not going out with your friends for Josie's birthday tonight."

Zoey mumbles under her breath, scrubs her face until it hurts, and hurries to get dressed. During Zoey's sophomore year of college she will go to Cancun for spring break and her friends will convince her that SPF 25 is enough to protect her pale body from the sun all day. Since she will have sworn off alcohol after a fraternity party gone wrong, she'll choose to stay out in the sun while most of her friends go back and forth to the bars. That night Zoey will be so sunburned and blistered that she'll have a panic attack. All she'll be able to hear is her mother's voice in her head yelling at her. She will imagine the splotches of skin cancer growing right before her eyes. The hotel doctor will give her a Valium, and she will wear long pants and a long-sleeved top for the rest of the trip.

In her history class, Katy stares at the clock over the doorway. She swears it is moving backward. Mr. Maron sits at his desk reading the *Orlando Sentinel*. Every few minutes, without looking up, he says, "Eyes on your own paper," "Don't make me move you," and his personal favorite, "Cheaters never prosper." Katy cannot understand why everyone is taking so long to finish the test. She handed hers in ten minutes ago, even though she couldn't think of the last freedom in the "four freedoms that America was founded upon." She can picture the page of her notebook where she had written them, but she can't make out the last one. She got the first three — freedom of speech, freedom of religion, and freedom from fear. Now as the clock ticks ever so slowly she realizes with a groan that the last freedom is freedom from want. She certainly doesn't have freedom from want right now, because what she wants more than anything is to trade the note from Josie's mother for her own note. Tomorrow, when Mr. Maron hands back the exams, Katy will discover she missed a whole page of questions, which accounts for why she had finished so fast.

Becky Dickson watches Josie hang her photograph on the clothesline without having rinsed it long enough. A few drops of fixative fall on the floor, leaving a small puddle that anyone could pick up with their shoe and track into their kitchen at home, where maybe their baby brother would crawl over it and then put his hand in his mouth. Josie doesn't even notice and walks right out of the darkroom. Becky wonders if Josie ever wonders why she isn't friends with her anymore. The two of them used to ride their bikes together after school until that day in seventh grade when Becky was at Josie's house and saw Josie's brother pick his nose and stick it under the kitchen table. Since then Becky has refused to step foot inside Josie's house. She would have given Josie an explanation if she had asked, but she never did.

No one ever notices the things that Becky does. They don't know so many important things. Like that scientists have found flesh-eating bacteria on pay phones. Flesh-eating! They don't know never to use the middle stall in a public restroom because it is the most germ-filled. Becky knows these things and more, but nobody listens to her. When she is thirty-three, with twin boys and an ex-husband, she will wash her hands so many times during the day that they bleed, and the doctor will diagnose her with obsessive-compulsive disorder. She will argue that she is not obsessive; she is just taking necessary precautions. Her therapist will be able to trace the onset of her condition to a documentary she saw when she was eleven, which used a special infrared camera to show the millions of microscopic bugs crawling over people's bodies as they go about their day.

Katy glares at the three students still holding onto their history tests. They don't seem to care that they are keeping her prisoner in this room. The clock is definitely moving backward. There is no other explanation for the eternal slowness of this class period.

Greg Adler is relieved that he has a little time to practice his *Haf* Torah during photography class. He can't believe his bar mitzvah is in two weeks. If it were up to him he wouldn't do it at all, but his grandfather would be really disappointed. At least now he'll finally become a man like he should have at thirteen. He didn't notice any of his friends from Hebrew school becoming any manlier, though, so he's not expecting much. But at least that pain in the ass Becky Dickson will stop making fun of him. He feels like he regresses to second grade when she talks to him.

Greg overhears Josie telling Tyson Davis that she needs to leave the room and wonders if he should explain why he was laughing at her picture. It was just so funny seeing Zoey holding this phallic-looking hot dog. After he'd kissed her that summer, she wouldn't even talk to him. It wasn't like he really minded. After all, she is so pale she looks like a vampire. A kind of cute vampire, though.

Mrs. Lombardo thinks she will never be able to sort through the stacks of paper piled on her desk like miniature skyscrapers. She unfolds the note from Josie Taylor and gives it a quick glance on its way into the filing drawer. Then she brings it closer to her face and reads it carefully. She pushes herself out of her seat and steps out of the office. She looks down the hall in both directions, but Josie is gone. She tucks the note into her pocket for safekeeping and then takes it out and reads it one more time.

Wiping away any traces of tears, Marissa Badish holds her head up high as she leaves the bathroom. She is embarrassed to have made such a scene in front of that sophomore. The girl was nice, though. Nicer than she would have been in her place. As she walks in a daze to her next class, she passes ultra-pregnant Sherri Haugen making her way slowly to her class. Her friend Val has to carry her books since she can't balance very well anymore. Marissa counts backward from the first day of her last period and hopes that her math is wrong. If she finds out she got knocked up like Sherri did, she'd lose her mind. Then she'd kill Steve. At lunchtime that afternoon, a relieved Marissa will find herself in the nurse's office looking for a tampon because the dispenser in the girl's bathroom is empty. Nurse Sanders isn't around, so Marissa will take one from the box on the shelf and vow never to have unprotected sex again. And she won't, until one afternoon twelve years later, when she will conceive a baby with Steve's cousin Kerry, whom she will have married because his face reminded her of Steve's, even though she swore to Kerry that it didn't.

In the gym locker room, Alyssa Levy pulls her t-shirt up over her head and unsnaps her bra. She watches as her breasts fall gently out of the cups. She wonders how long she will have them, since every woman in her family has had breast cancer. Only her mother and one aunt have beaten it by having their breasts removed before the cancer could get them. She is determined to enjoy hers for as long as she can and begins her daily stroll through the locker room, aware of the envious stares and storing them up for later, when the stares will be of pity instead.

Thirty seconds after the bell rings, Katy Parker runs into the school office. Before she can get any words out, Mrs. Lombardo reaches into her pocket, holds up the note, and says, "Is this what you're looking for?"

Chapter 4A: Josie

I sit down on the hard metal bleachers and wait for the rest of the class to get changed into their gym clothes. Jason Count enters from the boy's side. He looks even better than he did on the bus this morning. Maybe it's the tight gym shorts. I flip my hair over my shoulders and give him my best smile. He looks caught off guard but gives me a quick smile back. Then he looks away. I'm sure he's thinking, *Just what I need, one more girl with a crush on me.* And I don't even like him that much. I mean, I don't even know his class schedule!

Jason starts jogging around the track, his sneakers squeaking with each step. Admittedly, exercise is not my thing, but gym class has never made much sense to me. When am I ever going to have to climb a rope at top speed? To escape the clutches of a crazed lion? Or I'm sure some day I'll find myself in the middle of a circle trying to dodge a rubber ball being thrown at me from all sides. It's the same every day, no matter what sport we're playing: all the boys try to show off how athletic they are and the girls just try to avoid getting hit by the ball so we don't break a nail. Or maybe that's just me.

"Not joining us today, Josie?" Ms. Bitner asks. "You're not sick, I hope?" She does a set of lunges in front of me as she waits for my answer. I don't think I've ever seen her stand still for more than a few seconds at a time.

I shake my head. "I have to leave in a few minutes to take my driver's test. The office approved it."

Her lunges turn to squats. "Would you like to get in a few laps before you go?"

"Um, not really?"

"Okay," she says, reaching down to touch her toes. "But you should be sure to do some exercise today. Maybe jog a few miles after school."

"I'll try," I tell her, knowing for a fact it will never happen. Oddly enough, I don't think lying was on the list of seven deadly sins. But wait, *sloth* is, and I'd say being too lazy to exercise counts as sloth, so my homework is one-seventh done! Actually, it's more like three-sevenths done, if you count my *pride* in my appearance this morning in front of the mirror, and my *anger* at Katy for making me miss saying hi to Grant in the hall. Hmm. I'm moving through them at a remarkable speed. At this rate I'll be finished by lunchtime. I wonder if I should be concerned about this.

Ms. Bitner blows her whistle and everyone joins me on the bleachers for attendance. Katy is the last person out of the girls' locker room. She runs over with one sneaker still in her hand and sits next to me.

I lean close and whisper, "Where did you go before?"

She whispers back out of the side of her mouth, "I just had to take care of something."

"Is it about my birthday?"

Katy pauses. "Uh, sort of?"

"Cool."

"Here," Katy says loudly as Ms. Bitner calls her name. Then she points to a bulge in her sock and whispers, "I stuck my cell in there on vibrate. That way you can call me if you pass the driver's test."

"You think I might not pass?" I ask, instantly worried. If my best friend doesn't believe in me, what hope is there?

"I didn't mean it that way. I'm sure you'll pass, don't worry."

I can't help but worry. I only manage to parallel-park correctly half the time. I also don't know what to expect, since none of my friends have gotten their licenses yet. Katy and her long legs jog off to join the rest of the class for jumping jacks. I sling my bookbag over my shoulder and make my way around the jumping-jackers. As I pass Alyssa Levy I'm reminded of yet another of the seven deadlies that I've already committed. *Envy.* I'm really blowing through that list.

When I get to the front lobby, a boy I've never seen before is waiting as well. He nods at me as I set my bag down in front of the tall windows. We stand in silence for a minute and I sneak a glance at him. He has this expression on his face like he's thinking about something very deeply. My eyes wander over to a poster taped on the wall reminding the seniors not to bring their dart guns to school this week. I forgot Dart Wars starts after school today. It usually starts on the first Monday in March, but leap year must have pushed it back a day. I wonder if Rob signed up. Last year two kids were suspended for bringing their Nerf guns to school. Each year the principal tries to ban Dart Wars, but he never can. It's a tradition. The prize is five hundred dollars, but it's not really the money that matters. It's more the winning itself. The winners are famous for the rest of the year. I read the rest of the poster while I wait.

ONLY TWO PEOPLE TO A TEAM. NO SHOOTING ANYONE ON SCHOOL PROPERTY OR IN THEIR CARS OR AT THEIR PLACE OF EMPLOYMENT. NO NERF GUNS ANYWHERE ON DISNEY PROPERTY.

They left off the most controversial rule of all — you cannot be shot if you disrobe down to your underwear. It's not like they could write that on a poster in school. Everyone knows it anyway.

Suddenly the boy next to me gives a kind of half giggle, half shout. At first I actually think he knows I'm picturing someone stripping while a dart gun is aimed at him. I quickly realize that of course he doesn't know that. Just to be on the safe side, I move a few inches away and peer out the window for my father's car.

"Sorry," he says, turning to me. "Did I make a strange noise?"

"Pretty much."

"Sometimes I'm not sure if it's in my head or out loud."

"I know what you mean."

"Do you want to know what I was thinking about?" he asks.

I look at him in surprise.

"I was thinking about parallel universes. Are you familiar with them?"

"Not really." In the split second after I say this and before he responds, a strange jolt zips through my brain. I don't know what I was expecting him to be thinking about, but it sure wasn't parallel universes. I don't know why, but I always imagine that other people are thinking about really boring, mundane things. Why is it just hitting me on my sixteenth birthday that if I have weird thoughts, then other people probably do too? Is this something that everyone besides me knows?

"Let me explain, then," the boy says, his eyes bright. "The theory of parallel universes states that with every decision we make, there are an infinite amount of other choices that another version of ourselves is living out. So I was thinking that on some parallel Earth, some other version of me is standing right here, waiting for his mother to pick him up. Except this other me, he's going to town hall to get an award for outstanding service to his community.

That's why I was laughing. At least one of me is doing something good." He laughs again.

I smile at him. "So you're not going to town hall, I assume?"

"Oh, I'm going all right. But not to get an award, that's for sure."

I wait for him to elaborate but he doesn't. We stand in silence again. I look down at my watch. It's officially 10:45 and no Dad in sight. He's been so strange lately. At least I always knew where he was when he worked nine to five. Maybe something bad happened. An image of a tornado swirling out of the sky and flinging Dad's car into the air fills my head.

"What's your name?" the boy suddenly asks, dissolving the tornado image.

"Josie."

"I'm Mike Difranco. You going to the doctor or something?"

"Driver's test. I'm a little nervous."

"Don't worry, it's easy. Just watch out for that parallel parking. It's a doozy."

"Great," I say with a sinking feeling.

Mike suddenly looks excited. "Hey, does that mean it's your birthday today?"

"Yup."

"No way! You were born on Leap Day? That's awesome! Do you know how rare that is?"

I felt myself stand a little taller. "Yes, actually, I —"

"Sorry, gotta go, that's my mom," Mike says and two seconds later disappears through the door. I watch him climb into a red Toyota. As the car pulls away, my dad's car zooms into the circle in front of the school and screeches to a halt. I've never seen my dad screech before. I run out and hop in.

"I'm sorry I'm late, honey," he says as we take off. "I was reading about the history of Disney World."

"Boy, you must really be bored." But he doesn't look bored. There's a gleam in his eye I haven't seen very much of before.

"Did you know there are hundreds of Mickey Mouse designs hidden all around the parks?"

"No, Dad. I did not know that."

"Yup." He doesn't say anything else so I start daydreaming about an alternate me who lives in a parallel universe and who fails her test and hides in her closet in shame. As long as the alternate me fails, then the real me will have to succeed. It stands to reason. We slow down for a red light and I make a mental note of how close to the light Dad gets before he starts braking. When we come to a full stop he turns to me and asks, "You know how your mother and I always encourage you kids to follow your dreams?"

That's twice in five minutes that people have surprised me with what they ask. "Why is everyone asking me such weird questions lately? Do I have a sign on my back?"

"Who else asked you a weird question?"

"Some kid at school asked me if I'd heard of parallel universes. What were you saying about dreams?"

We're nearing the parking lot now for the Department of Motor Vehicles, and I should be focusing on my test. Instead, we're talking about dreams. This is not the way I thought this drive would go.

"If you had a dream, you'd want to pursue it, right?" Dad asks, keeping his eyes on the road. "Like how you love acting so much. You wouldn't let anything stop you, right?"

"I don't know, I guess not. Why? Do you know something I

don't know about the play? Tryouts aren't until this afternoon."
Then my heart starts to pound faster. Did Mr. Polansky call home
to tell my parents I wasn't going to get it? Was my father trying to
warn me?

We pull into a spot at the DMV, and Dad shuts off the car as my
heart continues to pound. "No," he says, "it's not about you."

I'm embarrassed, yet relieved. "Oh."

"Maybe we should talk about this afterwards. You have much
more important things to do right now than listen to me blabber on."

Before I can argue, he hustles me through the doors of the gray
brick building. It takes a few seconds for my eyes to adjust to the
gloom. Dad peers up at the different signs hanging from the ceiling
and motions me to the far right line.

"Who has a dream then?" I ask as we make our way through the
rows of hard plastic chairs. "Is this about Rob choosing which college to go to?"

He shakes his head. "You really need to focus now. Do you have
your information?"

I dig through my bag and find the folder where I put my birth
certificate and the card from driver's ed saying I passed the written
exam. Luckily three of the five people in line ahead of us were
actually standing in the wrong line, so we reach the front in only
a few minutes. The tired-looking woman behind the counter
holds out her hand, palm up, and I give her the two documents.
She enters some information in the computer and then goes to
use the photocopy machine. She doesn't appear to be an overly
happy person. In fact, as I look around, nobody seems very happy
to be here.

The woman returns and gives me my papers along with a small

orange form with my name printed on top. "Give this to your instructor," she says in a monotone voice and points me to a door on the other side of the building. "Wait there and someone will come get you."

We do as we're told and join two other kids and their parents. The girl is aggressively chewing on a cuticle. I'm afraid any minute she's going to start gnawing on her entire finger. The boy is staring straight ahead, shifting his weight from one foot to the other and back again. It's very rhythmic. Now that the time is almost here, my heart starts beating faster. I wonder if the swaying boy can hear it.

The boy's mother asks me and the other girl if our birthdays were yesterday, like her son's. The girl nods, still chewing, while I shake my head and tell her mine is today, Leap Day. I'm slightly disappointed when that evokes no reaction. A minute later a woman comes through the door and calls the girl's name. She looks panicked and doesn't move. Her father pushes her gently out the door. A minute later another woman comes and takes the boy and his mother. Now my hands are starting to get numb from anxiety. What if they can't grip the steering wheel? I flex my fingers and turn to ask Dad more questions, but he is very absorbed in a brochure called *Teens and Driving.*

A few minutes later an old man comes through the door and holds out his hand. Am I supposed to shake it? I hesitate and look at my dad. This guy is so old he probably gave my Dad *his* driving test! The man must sense my confusion because he sighs, holds up his clipboard, and says, "I need the orange form."

I quickly hand it to him. The tag on his jacket reads INSTRUCTOR, and below it, JOE.

"Follow me," Instructor Joe says and shuffles back through the door. He leads us to the curb and starts to get in the passenger side of a light blue car. I don't move.

"Aren't you coming?" he asks.

"Don't I take the test in my own car?"

He shakes his head. "Everyone uses the regulation cars now. Insurance issue."

I look pleadingly at my father. How could I do this in a different car? Dad's is the only car I ever practiced in besides the one at school, and that was so long ago.

"Isn't there any way she can use mine?" Dad asks the man.

He shakes his head. "No, sir. This one or nothing."

Alrighty then. I run around and slide in the driver's side. My father waits on the curb with his hands clasped tightly in front of him. I put on my seat belt and stare at the unfamiliar dashboard. For a second everything blurs and I'm afraid I'm going to cry. And I'm not a crier.

"Take a minute to get the lay of the land and let me know when you're all set," Instructor Joe says, shutting his eyes.

I take a deep breath like the driving instructor at school told us. Steering wheel. Lights. Horn. Gas pedal. Brake pedal. Odometer. Radio, probably won't need that. Emergency brake, *better* not need that. Rearview mirror. Side mirrors. Okay. I'm no longer on the verge of tears.

I tell him I'm ready and wait for instructions. He doesn't say anything, and finally I look over. His eyes are still shut and he's sitting very still. I wait another few seconds before it dawns on me that maybe Instructor Joe is *dead*! My hands start to sweat and I give the horn a little honk because I can't think of anything else to do. His eyes pop open and he asks me if I'm ready, as though he hadn't just returned from the grave. I wipe my palms on my pants and manage to nod.

The next few minutes are filled with: *Start the car, pull away from the curb, turn right, turn left, honk, turn on the wipers, do a K-turn, go in reverse.* I peek out of the corner of my eye at the marks he's making on his clipboard, but he keeps it close to his chest. My heart is pounding so loudly I'm sure he can hear it.

The only thing left now is the parallel parking. "Please maneuver the vehicle between those two orange cones," he tells me.

I approach the front cone and pull a half-car length ahead. I take another deep breath and slowly start backing the car into the spot. I realize too late that I'm about three feet away from the curb. I try to straighten out but it's no use. As a last-ditch effort I back up again and — *yikes* — hit the cone. Maybe he didn't notice? My heart sinks. I sit very still while he makes a lot of marks on the clipboard. I'll still pass as long as I didn't mess up anything else. I run the whole test back through my head. Did I remember to signal when I turned left? Did I check the rearview mirror before I backed up?

"You can drive back to the building now," he tells me.

I pull up to the curb, where my father is waiting, still wringing his hands. Instructor Joe undoes his seat belt and gets out. I follow straight away.

"Well?" my dad asks. "Did you pass?"

"I don't know yet." I turn to Instructor Joe and wait for him to say something. He makes a mark on the small orange form and hands it back to me. I look down. The box next to the word PASS has a checkmark in it.

"Oh, thank you, thank you!" I tell him, jumping up and down. Then, without really meaning to, I give the old man a hug. He doesn't hug me back, but he seems to soften a bit. I didn't let anyone down, that's the important thing.

"I knew you could do it, honey!" my father says, swinging me around. "Congratulations!"

Together we practically run back inside the office and wait in another line to hand in the form and get my license. The boy who was waiting with us before is at the front of the line, but I don't see the finger-chewing girl anywhere. I hope she's okay. It certainly feels different waiting in line now compared to before. Not only do I feel relieved, but I actually feel *older*. Josie Taylor, licensed driver. One scary thing down, two to go. But if tryouts go badly, I'm sure I won't even want to go to the lake.

When I hand in the form the woman types a few words into her computer. She double-checks my form again. "I'm going to have to manually type in your birthday, because the computer isn't recognizing it." She lumbers over to a desk and sits behind what must be one of the first typewriters ever made. I think of my leapmate Chris. No wonder his mother's doctor thought it would be easier to give him a normal birthday.

A minute later she's back and asks me to verify my name, address, height, weight, and eye color. I sign my name and she gestures for me to stand a few feet to the right to have my picture taken. Not surprisingly, there's no mirror on the wall. That would have been too thoughtful. I hurriedly smooth my hair down and hope there's no food in my teeth. Although if there was, it would have been there since breakfast, and that means no one would have mentioned it to me all morning and I'd be pissed.

I step onto the black *X* and before I even have a chance to smile, the woman clicks the button.

"Wait, can I try that again?"

She shakes her head. "Sorry."

I don't move off of the X. "Just one more time?"

The woman shakes her head and calls out, "Next."

I grumble and move off to the side. The next woman on line must be getting her old license renewed because she's at least ten years older than I am. As soon as she steps onto the X she breaks out into this huge smile. She clearly knows the score. While I wait for my name to be announced I call Katy and let it ring a few times to signal her. I sure hope she still has her cell on vibrate. Teachers will take your phone away if it rings during school. Five minutes later my name is called. I go up to yet another window.

"Congratulations," the skinny man behind the counter says with a big grin. He is the first person here who's in a good mood. He hands me the license. I'm afraid to look at it.

"Thank you," I tell him.

I hand it to my father. "You look, I'm too scared."

"Hey, this is a great picture!" he says.

"Really?" My heart leaps.

"No," he says, stifling a laugh.

"No?" I grab the license from him and force myself to look. My face is flushed and one eye is half closed. My lips are kind of puckered. I look like a sick fish.

"Hey, at least your hair looks pretty," he says.

I frown. "It's really awful, isn't it?" Then I start to laugh and my father leans over to look again.

"I've seen worse," he says as we head out to the car.

"When?"

He pretends not to hear me.

On the way back to school I stare at the license, struck by how official it looks. It looks even cooler when I cover my picture with my thumb. "Hey Dad, if you want, I can drop you at home and take the car back to school with me."

"No thanks," he says. "Besides, you're only insured to drive Grandma's car."

My parents still call the Shark *Grandma's car* even though she died eight years ago. Sometimes, when it rains, I can still catch a whiff of her White Shoulders perfume. "You added me to the insurance before I passed the test?"

"I told you I knew you could do it."

"I almost didn't. Did you see that parallel parking job?"

"I couldn't watch."

"I wish the instructor hadn't been watching."

We pull up to the school and I check my watch. Physics class should be almost over. "Thanks for taking me, Dad," I tell him, jumping out of the car. "Let me know when you want to finish that conversation about the dreams."

"Soon," he says. Then, "Wait, this came for you this morning from UPS." He hands me a box about the size of a regular tube of toothpaste.

I turn the box over in my hands. The postmark says "Boston." It must be from my leapmate Niki. I shove it deep into my bookbag. I'll open it at home. It will give me something to look forward to. As expected, the halls are empty when I get inside and it's a little spooky. Just me and the ghosts of students past. Maybe even poor Hunter Jr., who was lost before his time. I stop at my locker and grab my lunch. The door to my physics class is open so I peer in. The class is gathered around Mr. Lipsky's desk, watching some pulley-and-lever experiment. I enter as quietly as possible and set my bag down on my desk. I join the group and stand next to Zoey, who I am happy to see made it to school after all. I should probably tell her about the smudge of orange on the side of her neck, but I don't want to upset her.

As soon as she sees me she grabs my arm and asks in a loud whisper, "Did you get it?"

I nod, and she grips my arm even tighter and starts jumping up and down. "So the lake is on for tonight!" Between her fingers are more orange streaks.

"Yup." I'm starting to wonder if my friends are looking forward to this initiation more than I am.

"Can I see your license?" she asks when the experiment is over.

I quickly change the subject. "So I hear there was a self-tanning incident this morning?"

She nods. "I was as orange as, well, an orange. I looked like I came from another planet."

"Welcome to my driver's license picture."

"I'm sure it's not that bad."

"Trust me, it's that bad."

I open my notebook to get out my homework when Jeff Grand comes over and says, "So?"

I smile. "I passed."

He looks confused and then says, "Passed what?"

"My driver's test. What did you think I meant?"

His cheeks redden. "Actually I was talking about Katy. Did you tell her I wanted to ask her to the prom?"

Oops, I had totally forgotten about that. "I haven't told her yet. But you should know that only juniors and seniors can ask someone to the prom."

Again, he looks confused. "Oh, I didn't realize that."

"There's always the Spring Dance if you like her that much."

"It's not that I like her, exactly."

"Then why do you want to ask her to the prom?"

Jeff is apparently stumped by what should be an easy question. He gives his head a little shake and goes back to his desk. And women are supposed to be hard to figure out?

Chapter 4B: Everyone

Jason Count likes to be the first person in the gym and is surprised to see Josie Taylor sitting alone on the bleachers. He smiles back at her because it's the polite thing to do, but really he's thinking that he wishes he was alone and that he doesn't need one more girl to have a crush on him. Things are complicated enough with Emily. When they saw each other in the hall between first and second period, she barely spoke to him before running off with her friends. He can't understand why she would do that after all they'd been through the night before. He hasn't considered that she might be embarrassed. He thinks he must have done something wrong. He jogs around the perimeter of the gym, going over everything he has said to her since this morning on the bus. He is careful not to get too close to the bleachers so Josie won't think he's flirting with her. Twelve years later he will see Josie at their high school reunion, won't recognize her, and will ask her out.

Emily Caldwell's math teacher holds out her hand and waits for Emily to place her homework in it. Emily shakes her head. "Tomorrow, I promise."

Her teacher moves down the row and Emily lets her eyes flutter closed for a minute. She should have asked Jason to let her copy his homework. He has the same class this afternoon. She feels bad for having blown him off in the hallway earlier, but sometimes she can't stand the look in his eyes when he sees her. It's a combination of pity for her situation, anger at her father, and possessiveness. She wishes he could just look at her with love like she was a normal girl from a normal family where people don't get hit for spilling apple juice on the counter. She's tempted to break up with Jason just so she doesn't have to see that look anymore. But as much as she hates that look, she hates the idea of not having it more.

*   *   *

Katy hastily pulls her gym shirt over her head and kicks off her sandals. She still hasn't let go of the note Mrs. Lombardo returned to her. She keeps it in her hand while she slips her shorts on. When she's the last one in the locker room she pushes it deep into her bag and locks it in her small gym locker. She can't believe Mrs. Lombardo read it. Not that she did it on purpose, but it's just too embarrassing for words. She had told Katy not to worry, that her secret was safe. Katy slips on one sneaker, grabs the other, and says a little prayer that Mrs. L doesn't tell the person that the note concerns. She would just crawl into a hole and die.

That night Mrs. Lombardo will go home and call her older sister Ann-Marie in Chicago, whom she'll tell the whole story to. Together they will laugh until Ann-Marie threatens to pee in her pants. Mrs. Lombardo will never tell anyone else.

Out in the gym, Katy slips on her other sneaker and assures Josie that she'll definitely pass her driver's test. She crosses her fingers behind her back so Josie won't see that she's actually not so sure of that fact. Josie is a great best friend, but she's not such a great driver. The one time she rode in the back while Josie was practicing with her dad, Katy almost threw up from motion sickness. Josie tends to weave.

In the front lobby Mike Difranco taps his fingers against the window to a tune that's been running in his head all morning.

> I'm a cowboy
> on a steel horse I ride,
> 'cause I'm wanted,
> wanted,
> dead or alive.

His older brother is a big Bon Jovi fan. The oldies. Mike likes them too, but he prefers music you can dance to. Not that he would ever be caught dead (or alive) listening to it anywhere else than through his earphones. He could just picture what his brother would say if he heard techno coming out of Mike's stereo. It wouldn't be anything good, that's for sure.

A girl he's never seen before joins him in the front hall. She has very shiny hair. He nods hello. She probably has a dentist appointment, while he has to meet with Judge Philips again like a regular juvenile delinquent. He wishes he could change places with her. Not that he'd want to be a girl and deal with all that girl stuff like periods and makeup. But to be as innocent as she seems. *Ahhh, that'd be nice.*

Mike wishes he had never stolen that stupid bike, which even at the time he knew was too small for him. If only he could go back in time to last year before he knocked over his neighbor's lawn ornament and they called the police, or even further back to before his very first crime — throwing a rock into his other neighbor's window with a note tied around it professing his love for their daughter. He didn't mean to break the window. He was only eleven, but it started his reputation as a troublemaker. Maybe he could shift the universe a little and slip into a parallel one where he would be a good kid instead of a screw-up.

He chuckles at the thought of actually being lucky enough to fall into a parallel universe and the girl hears him. Not usually one to talk to pretty girls, he finds himself blabbering and it turns out she's nice. He's embarrassed to tell her where he's going. He decides if he wants to talk to more nice, pretty girls he'd better shape up.

Later at the courthouse in town hall, Judge Philips, who went to grammar school with Mike's mother, listens to Mike's earnest promise to turn over a new leaf and decides to give him one last chance. He assigns him to thirty hours of community service volunteering at either the children's hospital or the retirement home. Mike splits up the hours in each place and finds he likes helping people. In three years he'll join the Army, be promoted quickly through the ranks, parachute from a helicopter over an undisclosed location in the Persian Gulf, break both his legs, and get a purple heart. He will talk to many nice, pretty girls who would never believe he wasn't always an upstanding citizen.

Josie's father speeds through the streets on his way to pick up Josie at school. He almost never speeds, but today he's juiced up. He feels like a teenager again, even though he's about to take his own teenager to get her driver's test, a fact that blows his mind. How did his baby girl get to be sixteen already? He glances over at the dashboard clock and pushes slightly harder on the gas pedal. He hopes Josie passes her test today, although it might take a minor miracle. Hopefully the special magic of Leap Day will come through for her. If she does fail, she'd only have to wait three weeks before taking the test again. But he knows it would crush her. She puts on an air of confidence, but he suspects she's quite worried.

As Instructor Joe had anticipated, the girl he is assigned, Josie Taylor, grasps the steering wheel too tightly, not allowing it to glide through her hands on the turns. This causes the car to jerk slightly each time she straightens out. As soon as he tells her it's time for the parallel parking exercise, he knows she will fail it utterly. After thirty-six years on the job, little surprises him. He feels slightly nauseated after he gets out of the car, but he passes her anyway. He knew he would pass her even before they got in the car. She'll be just fine with a little practice. He knew she would hug him, too. They always do, the borderline ones.

As Katy walks to her next class she feels her left ankle vibrate. Katy smiles broadly. Two freshmen boys think she is smiling at them so they smile back. Katy doesn't notice. The party at the lake is on! She bends down and pulls the phone from her sock. As she drops it into her bag she makes a decision. Tonight she will come right out and tell Josie what she had written in the note. It is time. Let the pieces fall where they may.

*   *   *

Zoey keeps glancing up at the clock in her physics classroom. Josie should be getting back any minute. She can't stand the suspense. Zoey doesn't turn sixteen until October, and she envisions the four of them tooling around town in the Shark all summer, windows open, wind in their hair. Anything to get out of her house and away from her mother's prying eyes. She wishes her mother could be more like Josie's, who is very hands-off.

Finally Josie comes in the room and tells Zoey she passed the test. Zoey doesn't know if she's happier for Josie getting her license or that they'll all get to go to the lake. She can't wait to tell her brother, Dennis, that she'll need the blackberry brandy for tonight after all. Since Josie's going to be driving them around for the next few months, they better make her birthday really special.

Jeff Grand no longer remembers why he thought it was a good idea to ask Katy to the prom. He goes back to his seat after talking to Josie and puts his head on the desk. He always seems to mess up lately. It didn't used to be this way. He's too tired to figure out how to change things. That's the last thought he remembers having before the teacher, Mr. Lipsky, taps him on the head and tells him to wake up and stop drooling.

I bet the smell of our cafeteria is better than any other one across the country. For the last year, instead of unidentifiable gray meat and steamed vegetables and watery macaroni and cheese, we've had Taco Bell, Burger King, and Pizza Hut. One of the perks of living in Orlando is that stuff like this happens all the time. They explained to us that a marketing company is testing which menu items appeal the most to the teen demographic, or something like that. Disney is probably involved somehow. They're involved in everything else. My leapmates could not believe it when I wrote them about it. It's pretty darn cool. You can still buy the gray meat and watery macaroni, but nobody does.

Since I'll be getting my free Leap Day birthday pizza tonight, I opt for Taco Bell. As I reach for a tray someone tugs at my hair. It's Rob. His sidekick, Danny Daniels, is with him. With a name like Daniel Daniels, I suppose it makes sense that he's more than a little odd. Legend has it his father dared his mother to put that name down on his birth certificate. They're divorced now.

"Hey, li'l sis! How'd it go?"

"Get ready to share the car."

"That's great!" He hugs me. I'm glad I don't have one of those brothers who has to pretend to be all macho around me in public. Zoey's older brother only grunts at her in the halls.

"Jolly good job, ol' chap," Danny adds, tipping a pretend cap at me.

"Are you still being British?" I ask as I reach out for my Burrito Supreme. "Isn't that phase over yet?"

Danny is about to answer when he looks down at his feet. A

quarter lies on the ground between us. He reaches down for it and realizes too late that it is glued to the floor. "Bloody hell," he says, straightening up.

Rob and I laugh. "That's been there for two weeks," Rob says. "The oldest trick in the book."

Danny kicks at it with his foot but it doesn't budge. "Yeah? Well, Bob's your uncle!" he says, and heads toward the pizza line.

I ask Rob what the heck that means. He shrugs. "Some British expression. He says it when he can't think of anything else."

"Why are you friends with him?" I ask, only half serious.

"He's been my best friend since I was four. How many friends have I got?"

"A lot now. Remember? You're popular."

He shrugs. "It's not all it's cut out to be." He takes off after Danny and calls back to me, "Congratulations again!"

I pay for lunch and make my way through the tables toward the outdoor courtyard. The food selection is only one of the great things about lunch. The other great thing is that the sophomores and seniors have the same lunch schedule, so I get to see Grant. He always sits at the same corner table, but he's not there now. He brings his lunch from home, so he's usually seated already when I walk by. I casually glance around the cafeteria, making sure no one knocks into me and sends my burrito and soda flying. Three people wish me a happy birthday as they squeeze around me. It's nice to be remembered. As I'm waiting, I can't help noticing a pattern in the way people eat their lunches. The girls pull one item at a time out from their bags while the boys spread their stuff out like a feast. Someday someone will have to do a study on that. After a minute more I can't find any other excuse to stand in the middle of the aisle and am forced to give up on Grant.

Zoey and Megan are at our usual picnic table half underneath the tree by the fountain. It's a coveted spot. Zoey gets her shade and the rest of us slowly get tan. I'm about to lay my tray on the table when a plane roars overhead. It instantly makes me recall that last night I dreamed of a satellite falling. The dream had felt so real. I have to fight off the need to hide under the picnic table. I steady my grip on my tray until the plane finally passes. Megan slides her lunch of cucumber slices and water over to make room for me to sit. No one else even notices the plane, to say nothing of ducking from it.

"So?" Megan says, holding out her hand. "Let's see the evidence!"

"She won't show anyone," Zoey says, taking a bite of her Whopper.

"Why not?"

"She says it's not flattering."

"It isn't!" I insist.

Katy runs up to the table and throws her brown bag next to my tray. "Let's see it!"

Megan laughs. "Good luck."

"I look like a dead fish," I say weakly. Luckily at that moment Jenny Waxner, our class president, comes around with flyers and hands us each one. All it says is WWW.ORLANDOHIGHSCAVHUNT.COM AT 4 PM SHARP.

"The sophomore scavenger hunt is *today?*" Megan shrieks. "Why didn't we know this sooner?" Anything that cuts into Megan's rehearsal time for next month's *Beauty and the Beast* audition at MGM is barely tolerated. She almost wasn't going to try out for the school play, but I convinced her to do it. I'm hoping she lands the part of the nurse so she and I can have some scenes together. Assuming I'm Juliet of course. I refuse to consider any other outcome.

"The Sophmore Scav is always the same day as Senior Dart Wars," Jenny explains impatiently. "The list will go up at four, the hunt ends at six. On the dot."

Megan waves the flyer in front of Jenny's face. "But we haven't even signed up our team!"

"I signed the four of us up last month," Katy says. "I guess I forgot to mention it."

Jenny makes her exit as we turn to Katy in surprise. Katy has this photographic memory thing, where she remembers anything she reads.

"But Megan and I are trying out for the school play today," I remind her. "It starts during last period but it always runs another hour after school ends."

"So you'll still be able to get to my house by four, right? Okay, then, done deal."

Well, what could I say to that?

Zoey narrows her eyes at Katy. "What's been going on with you lately? It's not like you to organize something and forget to tell us."

"Nothing," she says, pulling a peach from her bag. "Why would you say that?"

"You seem out of it," Megan says. "Last night you were supposed to call me and you forgot. You never forget." Megan then looks pointedly at me. "What do you think, Josie?"

I chew thoughtfully on my burrito. I don't want to question Katy in front of everyone so I say, "She seems fine to me. Except for that whole note thing."

"What note thing?" Megan asks, leaning forward. She loves gossip, even when it's about her friends. Maybe especially when it's about her friends.

Katy looks at me pleadingly. We've been friends for so long that

I can pretty much read her mind. It's clear she doesn't want me to say anything, even though I'm not sure why. The lesson on improvisation in drama class kicks in, and I decide to practice my on-the-spot acting skills. "Oh, it's just some note we found in the gym locker room and Katy said we shouldn't read it. But I was like, sure we should, finders keepers, so we read it and it was all about 'I like this guy but he doesn't like me, I'll just die if he doesn't ask me to the Spring Dance, boo hoo.'"

Katy has a half-amused, half-grateful look on her face.

Megan's eyes widen. Zoey stops mid-bite and, mouth full of burger, asks, "Who wrote the note?"

Katy kicks me under the table before I can respond. She says, "Sadly, that part was torn off."

"I bet it was that girl Alyssa —" Zoey begins, then suddenly stops talking and jumps up off the bench. She points across the lawn. "Oh my god, Sherri Haugen is finally going into labor!"

We all whirl around. Sure enough, a whole crowd has formed around the blanket where Sherri Haugen always sits with her crowd of friends.

"Give her room," one of her girlfriends yells. "Everyone clear away!"

No one moves. "Get out of the way!" a louder voice calls out. It is Nurse Sanders. She huffs and puffs through the courtyard. Two of the school security guards scurry behind her, carrying a stretcher.

"How'd they find out so fast?" Megan asks without turning her head away from the action.

"Maybe they were watching from a window," Katy suggests.

The crowd parts and we watch them lift Sherri onto the stretcher. They must be strong, because she is huge. She's the only pregnant person I've ever seen close up, so maybe it's normal to be so huge. She must weigh two hundred pounds, though. By this time an ambulance has arrived and they carry her toward it. Her girl-friends surround her on both sides, smoothing her hair and holding her hands while she whimpers.

"Where's her boyfriend?" Zoey asks.

We look around. Usually Bobby's not more than a foot away from her at all times. We don't see him anywhere.

"I hear she's giving the baby up for adoption," Megan whispers.

Katy shakes her head. "I heard she's keeping it and getting married."

We sit back down and resume eating. I have no idea what I would do in Sherri's place. I intend never to have to find out. At that moment the always-annoying Missy Hiver leans over from the next table. "You guys don't know anything," she says. "Sherri and Bobby broke up last week."

"How do you know that?" I ask.

She purses her lips. "Despite what you might think," she says, "I'm not stupid. I hear things just like everyone else."

"I never said you were stupid."

"Right," she says. "Whatever." With that she turns around and keeps her back to me.

"What was that all about?" Megan asks. "What does that girl have against you?"

"I have no idea." I hate to admit it, but it's starting to bother me. As much as I don't understand why people *do* like me, it still annoys me when they don't.

"Well, we all love you," Zoey says, patting me on the back. "Even if you do closely resemble a dead fish!"

I look up from my root beer and see to my horror that Zoey is holding up my license so the other three can see it. All at once they cover their mouths and laugh. Zoey must have snuck it out of my bookbag while we were watching the Sherri saga unfold. I make a grab for it, but she holds it high above her head.

"It's not so bad," Katy says. "Hey, and now you can drive for the scavenger hunt this afternoon."

"Are you kidding?" I tell her, making another grab for the license. "You want me to drive all over town on my very first day behind the wheel?"

"She's right, Josie," Megan says. "We need someone on the team with a car. We could always ask Missy, she has her license and I bet no one else wants her! How 'bout that?"

I turn to Katy. "You knew I'd have to drive when you signed us up, you bad, bad friend."

"Cheer up," Megan says. "If we get killed, at least we'll all die together."

"I can't die on my birthday anyway," I mutter under my breath. Although I can still be maimed and bruised.

"Here," Zoey says, "you can have this back." She holds out the license and I grab it. "We're not really making fun of you. We're just jealous." Before I push it far down into my bag, I take one last look and shudder. When I turn back to my burrito there's a candle in it. The three of them break into the happy birthday song. I'm about to blow out the candle when I see Rob and his girlfriend, Anne, hurrying across the lawn to his car. *Our* car now. Anne is a few steps ahead of him. I turn back to the candle and briefly consider wishing that someday I'll be the one stealing away to kiss someone in the Shark. In the end I decide to wish that a magic bubble would form over the heads of everyone I love to protect them from things that fall from the sky.

I pull the candle out of the burrito and stick it in the side pocket of my bag, where I find the second muffin my mother gave me. It's still fairly intact.

"I forgot, my mother made this for you." I hold the muffin out to Megan with the least-crushed side facing her.

She eyes it hungrily, but in a split second her expression changes to one of horror. "Do you know how much butter is in a homemade muffin?"

"A lot?"

"Belle would never eat that."

"But Belle loved a beast," Zoey says. "She doesn't care about things like outside appearances."

Megan nibbles on her cucumber slice. "Yeah, but you didn't see her complaining too much when the beast turned into a handsome prince."

Katy reaches across the table and takes the muffin from my hand. "Anything your mom makes is bound to be good."

"Such a suck-up," Megan mutters.

Katy grins with the pieces of muffin stuck all in her teeth.

The bell rings and I stuff the last bite of the burrito into my mouth. I think I could live happily on Taco Bell forever. After agreeing to meet at Katy's house for the Scav, Megan and I head off to world religions class. It finally hits me that she's wearing an extremely Juliet-like peasant blouse.

I turn to her. "You're still trying out for the nurse, right? Not Juliet?"

She nods. "Absolutely. This was just the only clean thing I had."

When we pass the bathroom, Megan tells me she has to go and that she'll meet me in class.

"I'll come with you," I offer.

"That's okay. I'll just meet you." She pushes the bathroom door open before I can answer.

She probably has a stomachache and wants privacy. When I get to the classroom I help move the desks into a circle the way Ms. Connors likes it. Suddenly a thought hits me like a ton of bricks — Megan goes to the bathroom an awful lot. Is she throwing up her lunch? She barely ate anything to begin with. When she gets to class I examine her as closely as I can without being obvious. Her face is a bit flushed, but that could be from hurrying to class. Couldn't it? I'm going to have to pay closer attention.

Once again, I've forgotten to tell Katy about Jeff Grand's prom invite. Argh.

Danny Daniels watches his friend Rob hurry into the cafeteria. "Wait up, ol' chap!" he calls out. Rob doesn't hear him, or pretends not to. He's too focused on finding Anne. Even though Danny likes Anne, he doesn't like having to share his best friend. Plus, Danny thinks that having a girlfriend is more trouble than it's worth. You have to buy them things, take them to dinner, tell them that their new jeans don't make them look fat, and you can't look at other girls while they're around. Anne's probably outside with her friend Sherri, the one that quiet kid Bobby knocked up. It's always the quiet ones. Yet another reason not to have a girlfriend.

Danny catches up with Rob and they sneak up on Rob's sister, Josie. Danny thinks Josie is cool. He read once that all little sisters have a crush on their brother's best friend. When he can't pick up the quarter he feels like an idiot. He shouldn't have tried for it, it's just that every cent counts these days. His father shouldn't have backed out of his offer to send him to England this summer to visit him and his new wife. Danny is determined that he'll get there on his own. He doesn't know that the reason his father cancelled the trip was because his new wife hadn't told her family that Danny's father had been previously married. Danny will work double shifts at The Gap for the next four months before he finds out the truth. He'll pretend it doesn't matter, but after that he will no longer say "pip pip" or "jolly" anything. Six years later he will go to graduate school outside London and will look up his father's family. He will learn he has a half brother. Danny's father will introduce him to his new family as "a second cousin from the States." Another six years will pass before Danny forgives him.

Mitch Hurley watches Josie as she stands by the door of the courtyard and looks around the cafeteria. She's trying not to be obvious, but he knows whom she's looking for. You always know who the girl you like likes. Mitch is glad that Grant will be graduating this year. The guy's a jerk but he tries to act like he's not. Even though Mitch's mother made him take down the pictures of Josie, he still likes to think he knows the location of all the freckles on her face. He'd bet his left arm that Grant doesn't even know she *has* freckles. When Mitch is nineteen and home from college for the summer, he will find himself at the same pool party as Josie. By that time, he'll have a girlfriend named Marcy who has heard all about his childhood crush. Marcy will bet Mitch that he's still too chicken to approach Josie. Mitch proves he's not by marching straight up to Josie and saying hello. Josie will welcome him with a big hug and Marcy will fume in the corner of the hot tub for the rest of the party.

Grant parks in front of the lawyer's office. He turns to Bobby and asks, "Are you sure you want to do this?"

Without hesitation, Bobby says, "Yes. Sherri and I really think this is best for everyone." He pauses for a second and then says, "You can wait in the car if you want."

"No, I'll come in." He never thought he'd be accompanying Bobby to sign a form that would release a baby for adoption. He never thought Bobby would get anyone pregnant. He never thought Bobby would ever have a girlfriend. Bobby was always quiet and kind of dorky, really. Grant has only been friends with him all these years because their mothers play bridge together. He was surprised that Bobby had asked him to come, but he knew his mother would be pissed if he said no.

Bobby scribbles his name at every X without even reading the document. He knows he won't have to put down the final signature until after the baby is born in a few weeks. He also knows that Grant is only here out of a sense of duty. Bobby couldn't care less; he just needed a ride. He sold his car six months ago to help Sherri pay for doctors and stuff. Her parents' insurance didn't cover everything. He guesses he's pretty lucky that her father didn't come after him with a shotgun and demand they get married. Once Sherri decided she didn't want to have an abortion, they agreed that giving the baby up for adoption was the best option. This way a family who really wants a baby will get one.

Zoey and Megan arrive at the lunch table at the same time. "Did you ask Dennis about the beer yet?" Megan asks.

"I thought we were getting blackberry brandy."

"Whichever."

"I saw him on the lunch line and told him. He said he'd give us one bottle, but it's a big one. He has a whole case of it under his bed."

They take turns glancing up to see if Josie is coming. "Have you tasted it?" Megan asks.

Zoey nods and crinkles her nose. "It's pretty nasty."

"We'll only need a little."

Sitting cross-legged, Sherri Haugen lifts the box of Junior Mints to her mouth and shakes it a bit. As she tastes the chocolatey goodness of the first mint, she is suddenly aware of a drip of water between her thighs. By instinct, she squeezes them closer together. This whole peeing-at-random thing is one of the worst parts of pregnancy. Then again, the humiliation of being a statistic, the farting, and the getting fat aren't so great either. At least it's almost over and then her life can get back to normal. She shifts on the blanket and feels even more moisture between her legs. Squeezing her legs isn't working. The drip has turned from a dribble to more like a gush.

"Um, Sherri?" her friend Val says. She points to a wet spot on the blanket next to her that is growing bigger and bigger. "Is that normal?"

"Oh my god," Sherri says, staring at the puddle. "I think my water just broke."

"But your due date isn't for another two weeks!" Val squeals, jumping up.

"Tell that to the baby," Sherri replies, her voice quivering. She reaches for her pager and types in SHERRI 911. The message immediately goes out to three preprogrammed numbers.

Nurse Sanders is just about to take the first sip of her strawberry-banana smoothie when her beeper goes off. She yanks it off her hip and squints to read the message. She tosses the beeper on the desk and makes a call to the two security guards on duty. Two minutes later she is clearing the crowd away from the lawn. She had warned Sherri that young girls often give birth a few weeks early, but Sherri insisted on staying in school until the last minute. When she reaches Sherri, Nurse Sanders can see that her water has broken. Sherri looks at her with a wide-eyed panic usually reserved for tornado warnings. Her girlfriends clearly don't know what to do either. She is lucky her friends have stood by her. When Nurse Sanders was growing up, if a girl got in the "family way," everyone steered clear of her like it was contagious.

"You sure you aren't having twins?" she asks Sherri as the two men lift her onto the stretcher.

Sherri glares at her. She was just trying to lighten things up a bit. She pulls Sherri's friends to the side. "Go with her," she tells them. "Try to keep her calm."

"I can't go," one of them says frantically. "I have a math test."

Nurse Sanders puts her hands on the girl's shoulders. "Your friend here is about to give birth. You can make up your math test."

The girl nods, her eyes wide.

"I'll let the office know y'all left for the day. Now scram."

Bobby and Grant are almost back at school when Bobby's beeper goes off. He takes one glance at it and reaches out blindly for the wheel. The car swerves.

"Hey, what the heck are you doing?" Grant shouts as he straightens out the car.

"It's Sherri! She's in labor. You have to take me to the hospital!"

"Now? But I —"

"Now," Bobby says. "Right now!" He makes another grab for the wheel but Grant holds his arm out to stop him.

"Calm down! I'll drive you there." He turns the car around in the 7-Eleven parking lot and heads up toward Orlando Regional Hospital.

"Where are you going?" Bobby asks, gesturing frantically.

"To the hospital!"

"You're going the wrong way! She's at Eastside!"

Grant groans and veers into the parking lot of Best Buy, where it's illegal to make a U-turn. He does it anyway. Five blocks later he hears the sirens.

"Don't stop!" Bobby says. "She'll kill me if I'm not there when she arrives!"

Grant pulls over and Bobby starts getting antsy in his seat. The policeman comes to Grant's window and looks in. Before he can ask for Grant's license and registration, Bobby leans over and says, "Pleaseofficerwehavetogettothehospitalmygirlfriendishavingababy!"

The policeman ignores him. He probably thinks they are trying to get out of a ticket.

"License and registration, please," he says to Grant. As Grant opens his wallet for his license, Bobby gets out of the car.

"Please, officer," Bobby pleads. "You've got to believe me."

"Get back in the car," the cop says. Then he sees the crazed look in Bobby's eyes. "You're not kidding, are you?"

Grant leans out of his window. "No, he's not."

"Okay," the policeman says. "Go on back in the car, I'll give you an escort."

Bobby runs back to the passenger door and calls out, "Eastside!"

Missy Hiver can't help but overhear Josie and her friends speculating about Sherri Haugen and her boyfriend, Bobby, and the future of their baby. She always wanted to start a rumor and now is her chance. She thinks about it for a second and then tells them she heard the couple broke up. She turns back to her table with a Cheshire Cat grin on her face. Now all she has to do is wait to see how far the rumor spreads by the end of school today. If she's caught she'll just say Josie made it up.

"Anne, wait up," Rob calls out, but Anne keeps hurrying through the parking lot. She stops at the side of the Shark and waits for him to get there. Then she says, "We have to talk."

They get in the car and sit in silence, staring out the windshield. Rob is starting to panic. "What's going on? You're scaring me."

"Did you see how they just took Sherri away?"

"Yeah, so?"

"She's about to have a baby!"

"Anne, we've known that since last summer."

"I can't do this anymore," she says, an edge of hysteria in her voice.

"Do what?" Rob's heart starts beating faster. He swears he can feel it in his temple.

"This," she gestures around the car. "This, us, sex, the whole thing."

"Fine, done, no more sex. We only did it once anyway."

"It's not just that," she says. "I'm not ready for a serious relationship. I thought I was, but when I saw Sherri today, something just snapped. I'm sorry, Rob, I'm really sorry."

"We can slow down," he says, reaching for her hand. "That's not what I care about."

For a second her expression softens, and he feels a rise of hope. But then it passes and she slips her hand out of his grasp. "I'm sorry, Rob. You're a great guy, really." She reaches for the door handle.

He feels like a deflated balloon as he watches her get out of the car, possibly for the last time ever. "If I'm so great, why are you doing this?"

She leans in the window. "I hope we can be friends."

Rob watches her walk away. Her and her strawberry lip balm and her kindness and her laughter. He feels a pain in the center of his chest and presses against it. Now he knows why they call it heartache. His heart actually physically aches. The lunch bell rings, and he slowly opens the door into an empty parking lot.

Megan leaves Josie and darts into the last stall of the bathroom. She taps her foot as she waits until some girl finishes washing her hands and leaves. Then she dives into her backpack and pulls out half of a salami sandwich and a Hostess cupcake wrapped in tin foil. She would have rather had one of Josie's mom's homemade muffins, but this will have to do. She wolfs the sandwich in six bites. Josie is so dedicated to being an actress, and Megan doesn't want her to think she's any less dedicated. Actresses are supposed to watch their weight. Everyone knows that. For about one second she debates saving the cupcake for later. Four bites later it's gone. *Mmm mmm.* A little slice of heaven.

I watch as Ms. Connors tacks another quote onto the big bulletin board. Every Monday there's a new one. Today's is: "In life there are no make-up exams. Choose wisely." I glance hard at Megan. Last week's quote was "Don't trust anyone over thirty." That one was kind of a joke, though, because Ms. Connors turned thirty last week.

Ms. Connors takes her seat and slowly scans around the circle, meeting everyone's eyes. That's her way of taking attendance. She says the eyes are the windows of the soul, and she can tell if we're truly here or if we're zoned out somewhere. At first it was weird having this teacher look at you so deeply, but now I don't mind. Ms. Connors is so cool that you almost feel like she really cares about you. And since she kind of looks like Gwyneth Paltrow, I bet more than one boy has a crush on her. I always thought she'd make a much better match with Mr. Simon than that uptight Ms. Robinson. I mean, if he *had* to choose someone other than me.

Ms. Connors passes around a pile of brochures and announces, "The guidance office asked all sixth period teachers to distribute this to our classes. They'll be starting a series of voluntary discussion groups. Take a minute now to look this over, and if you're interested in any of them, drop the form off at the guidance office before your next class."

The front of the brochure has a picture of a group of kids sitting around in a circle, like we are now. I don't recognize any of them, though. They all have big 80s hair. In fact, they're wearing sweaters, something we'd never wear down here. The brochure explains that the groups will be held once a week during regular class periods and are completely confidential. So I'd get out of class for this? I scan the list of groups, almost hoping I'll find something. *Family Issues, Drugs and Alcohol, Grief and Loss, Eating Disorders* (again, I glance at Megan, who actually looks happy, not like she just threw up, which I take as a good sign, unless she's happy with herself for throwing up, in which case it's a bad sign), *Abusive Situations, Depression, Relationships, Stress, Sexual Identity, Moving, Pregnancy, Divorce, Academic Problems, Peer Issues, Self-Esteem, Anger Management,* and *Attention Deficit Disorder.* I can't believe how many problems I could have right now!

"Did everyone complete the homework assignment?" Ms. Connors asks.

Most people nod, a few look down at their desks. That's one thing about sitting in the circle; no one can hide.

"Any volunteers?"

As usual, my hand shoots up. Ms. Connors looks around the circle hoping someone else will volunteer. Greg Adler starts to raise his arm and then lets it sink back down. I think he feels a little self-conscious being the only Jewish person in the class. When we started the chapter on Judaism, Ms. Connors asked him to talk about his upcoming bar mitzvah. He had to explain that he had mono at thirteen, which is why he's just having his bar mitzvah now. One kid asked, "Isn't mono the kissing disease?" Greg's face turned bright red and stayed that way for eleven minutes. I counted.

"How about you, Sara?"

Good luck with that one. Sara Beron has barely said anything in class for the last few months. She's always been quiet, but lately even more so. Sara shifts in her seat and slightly shakes her head.

My hand is still up.

"Okay, Josie. What Yiddish expression did you find?"

I hold my notebook close to my face to make sure I'm reading it correctly. "*Mit dyna kiskas feldor zholen mestin*. May they measure fields with your intestines."

The class laughs. Even Sara cracks a small smile. The quote was the first one I'd come across in my Internet search. I hadn't really thought about how gross it was until just now. It's also not very nice.

Just then a loud ringing comes through the loudspeaker, and we all jump a little in our seats. It's the fire alarm.

"Okay, everyone," Ms. Connors says, standing up. "Leave your stuff here. Let's go, and quietly."

I love fire drills. They're an unexpected bonus. Like finding a crumpled dollar bill in your jeans pocket or one last McDonald's french fry in the bottom of the bag. We file into the hallway and join the rest of the throng. We're supposed to be totally silent, and the bell is just so darn loud that it's not hard to comply. Each class is supposed to stick together, but once we're outside everyone gravitates toward their friends. Megan goes off to find Zoey and I wander around in search of Katy. I can't help it if I keep my eyes open for Grant too. He must have gone home sick or something; I just don't see him anywhere. Megan and Zoey have found each other and laid claim to one of the benches in the shade. God help Zoey if she came home with even a slight tinge of pink on her skin. When I approach they immediately jerk their heads apart.

"Oh, it's you," Zoey says.

"Nice greeting," I reply, positioning myself between them.

"We were plotting an ice cream run and didn't want anyone to hear," Zoey explains in a loud whisper.

"We can't leave school during a fire drill!"

"We won't have to," Megan says. "We could get it from the

freezer in the cafeteria since everyone is outside right now. It's not like I even want to eat it, I just want to see if we can do it."

"But the fire drill's almost over," I point out. "We'll get caught."

"I don't think so," Zoey says. "Listen."

In the background we can hear the fire engines approaching from a few blocks away. That means the fire department was called to check everything out and it isn't a scheduled drill. Someone must have pulled the alarm. Unless there's a real fire, but somehow I doubt that. It could be a while and it is really hot out here and I really *could* use an ice cream sandwich. "Let's do it."

We stand up and I do a quick scan for Katy. I find her standing near Ms. Connors and some of the kids from my class. She must be looking for me. I tell the others to wait and go pull Katy away. She glances back at Ms. Connors.

"Don't worry," I tell her. "She won't notice I'm not with the class."

"Are you sure?"

"Do you think your teacher cares where you are?"

"Good point. Where are you taking me?"

"You'll see."

We join Zoey and Megan and casually make our way to the edge of the crowd. A few seconds later we've made it around the corner of the building and into the empty courtyard where we'd finished lunch less than an hour ago.

"Shouldn't someone stand guard?" Megan asks.

Zoey shakes her head. "It's not like we'd hear you from here if you yelled anyway."

Megan looks relieved. I don't think she wanted to wait on her own. I know I wouldn't.

We push through the doors and run across the cafeteria. The

tables still have scraps of food on them. It's very weird being in here, just the four of us. Almost like I'm in the middle of a dream where everyone has suddenly disappeared except for my friends and me. We reach the freezer with the ice cream and stop in front of it.

"We're stealing ice cream?" Katy asks. "That's what you brought me here for?"

"Is theft one of the seven deadly sins?" I ask.

At the same time they all say, "Huh?"

"No, but gluttony is," a female voice replies from behind the counter. My heart jumps into my throat. One of the staff must not have left the building. We whirl around and come face to face with Amelia from my English class and super-shy Sara from world religions. Together they must have ten ice cream sandwiches between them. No one says anything as we stare across at each other. Amelia has this mischievous expression on her face. She's so good at it she must have practiced it in front of a mirror. Sara looks like a deer frozen in headlights.

Megan reaches for the freezer door and pulls on it. It's locked.

"Say not a word," Amelia warns us in a low voice. My friends and I back slowly away from the freezer. I'm too surprised to say anything even if I wanted to. Now I really feel like I'm in some sort of bizarre dream. The two of them stuff the sandwiches in the plastic bag Sara is holding and start heading back through the table area.

"Hey, Sara!" Megan calls out. Sara stops in her tracks and Amelia glares at both of them. Sara, not surprisingly, doesn't answer.

In a sweet voice Megan asks, "Can I have an ice cream?"

Sara haltingly reaches into her bag but Amelia grabs her by the t-shirt and pulls her away.

For a second the four of us don't move. Then Megan calls after them, "May they measure fields with your intestines!" We turn toward each other and burst out laughing. I laugh so hard that I actually have to hold the sides of my stomach. Zoey leans against the freezer and wipes tears away from her eyes.

Just then the fire alarm bell gives off a short ring, signaling that everyone can go back inside. We head toward the door that leads into the hall, planning to blend in with the rest of the crowd. I ask if anyone else thought Amelia sounded possessed.

"Maybe Amelia is possessed by the ice cream demon," Katy suggests, still breathing hard from the laughing.

"And how did she rope poor Sara into helping her?" I ask.

"What's wrong with that girl?" Katy asks. "Why didn't she say anything?"

"Ah, that's the big mystery," Megan says. We part ways at the water fountain and Megan and I hurry to catch up with our class. That kid Mike who I was waiting in the front hall with this morning is walking toward us. He winks at me as he gets closer. I wonder if he was the one who pulled the fire alarm. As we pass each other I turn my head and look at him. He turns, too, and shakes his head with a smile. I guess he knew what I was thinking. There's more to that kid than meets the eye.

When we get back to our class, Sara is already in her seat. The bag of contraband is nowhere in sight. We have only five minutes left to the period and then it's time for the auditions. I can't decide if I wish time would hurry up or slow down. Speed up so I can be on that stage. But slow down so I don't have to worry about blowing it. The minutes tick on. Once everyone has settled in, Megan raises her hand. I hope she's not going to ask to go to the bathroom again.

"Yes, Megan?"

Megan looks directly at Sara and asks, "Ms. Connors, do some religions believe people can be possessed by demons?"

"Why do you ask?"

"Oh, no reason. Just wondering. Like if someone does something that you wouldn't think they would do."

"Well," Ms. Connors says wearily. "Demonology is a bit out of the realm of the class curriculum. Suffice it to say, it's not a big part of modern religion."

"But on *Buffy the Vampire Slayer* —" Megan begins.

Ms. Connors holds up her hand to stop her. "Do you have a Yiddish saying for us today, Megan?"

Megan reluctantly opens her notebook. "My grandfather said he remembered an old man on his street in Brooklyn saying this to the neighborhood butcher, who ripped him off: 'May you fall from the top of the Chrysler Building and may people lean out their windows and hit you on the head with a baseball bat as you go by.'"

The class laughs. A colorful bunch, those Yiddish folks.

The bell rings and Megan and I are the first to run out of the room. We take off in different directions since we both have to run to our lockers before tryouts. I flip open my locker and pull the plastic brush off the shelf. Squinting in the small mirror on the inside of the door, I run the brush through my hair with one hand and put on lipstick with the other. A minute later I'm hurrying down the hall to the auditorium where the tryouts are going to be held. I'm about ten feet away when someone bumps into my left shoulder. I spin around. It's Grant Brawner. I'm so surprised that my mouth doesn't seem to want to work properly. I guess he didn't go home sick after all.

"Oh, sorry, Josie," he says, picking up the books that he dropped. "I wasn't watching where I was going."

I try to form the words, "That's okay," but what comes out is more like a squeak.

"Well, see ya," he says and walks away.

Many thoughts crowd my head as I struggle to focus on walking the rest of the way. Here they are, in order:

1. How stupid am I that I couldn't say anything?
2. HE CALLED ME BY NAME! He usually just says hi, if he says anything at all.
3. Maybe he'll ask me to the prom!
4. How stupid am I to think he'd ever ask me to the prom?
5. If I get the role of Juliet, he'll have to ask me for my picture again for the playbill!
6. If I don't get the role of Juliet, he'll ask SOME OTHER GIRL for her picture, fall in love with her, and take HER to the prom.
7. He sort of smelled like he needed a shower.

Ms. Connors has only a few minutes before her sophomore world religions class files in. She sorts through her pile of quotations for the right one to post today. Will these words of wisdom inspire her students to be better people? Will the quotes make them look at the world around them a bit differently? Sometimes she lies awake at night, alone in her double bed, afraid she'll never be able to teach them the things they'll truly need to know about life. Can she teach them how to repair a broken heart? Or explain that it never really gets repaired, just scarred over? How will she teach them to watch people they love die from old age or worse? How to pick the right job, the right mate? How can she convince them that every day there are little gifts to find in surprising places, that they just have to keep their eyes open? She loves teaching world religions, because she gets to pick the best lessons each tradition has to offer. As an agnostic, Ms. Connors doesn't know if there is one god, a trinity of gods, a thousand gods, or none at all. She knows only that it is her job to spark the spirit within each and every student. It frustrates her to no end that she can never tell if it's working.

Sara Beron likes being the first one in a room. Even though Ms. Connors is there, she is busy at her desk, so Sara doesn't have to worry about anyone trying to strike up a conversation. Everyone thinks it's this big mystery that she doesn't talk very much. She's heard the theories. She was attacked in a dark alley, aliens abducted her and swore her to silence, she witnessed a murder, she wants attention. The school psychologist literally got down on her knees and begged for her to talk. Sara felt a little guilty about that, because the woman tore her panty hose and didn't get any information out of her. It's not like she's mute or anything cliché like that. She ordered a pizza over the phone last night with no problem. She couldn't do that if she were mute.

At this point, the only person she'll willingly talk to is her cousin Amelia, even though Amelia isn't exactly her favorite person in the world. She's afraid if she talks to anyone for too long she'll blurt out what she saw. What she saw was this: her mother kissing the bagboy at Publix Supermarket. It was Christmas break and Sara and Amelia had stopped in there to get some ice cream because the Baskin Robbins was temporarily closed for remodeling. Amelia's parents are really religious and don't allow her to have things like ice cream. They say that eating for pleasure goes against something in the Bible. That doesn't stop Amelia, though. Once inside the market they had decided to split up and each find the grossest thing in the store, then dare the other person to eat it. Sara was about to pick up the freezer-wrapped cow's brains when she spied her mother's familiar blond ponytail at the end of the frozen dinners. She was about to call out her name when she saw this man — boy, really — swing her mom around. Her mother giggled and pulled him to her. He leaned her up against the frozen doors and they kissed, really passionately. Like in the movies. Sara tried to tear her eyes away but she couldn't. The shock felt like an ice pick stabbing her brain. If this had really been a movie, her father would come running in to separate them. But he didn't. A spill in aisle four finally broke the spell, and Sara ran to find her cousin.

"I dare you to eat this!" Amelia said, holding up fresh frog legs marinated in balsamic vinaigrette.

"We have to go," Sara answered, grabbing her cousin by the arm. She didn't talk all the way home, but that was because she was in shock. When her father opened the door with his usual big, goofy grin, she was petrified she would tell him. She was afraid that if she did, her parents would get a divorce and it would be her fault. Sara thinks Amelia actually likes the fact that she won't talk to anyone else. Amelia sees it as the ultimate rebellion, which it isn't.

Megan is the last person to get to Ms. Connor's class. She can still taste the cupcake left over in her molars. It makes her happy. She is unaware that

Josie is staring at her, wondering what accounts for the warm pink glow on her face. She would never imagine doing what Josie is silently accusing her of. She has a much too healthy appreciation of her body. Her body is her temple and she treats it as such. Every night she fully exfoliates all the dead skin on her arms and legs with a pumice stone. Then she liberally applies watermelon-scented body lotion, paying careful attention to her hands. When she was ten, her favorite baby-sitter told her that a woman's age as she gets older is revealed by her hands. Megan figures it's never too soon to start protecting her skin, especially for an actress/ singer like herself.

Greg Adler raises his hand to share his Yiddish expression, but changes his mind midway. He hates knowing that everyone in the class is aware of his religion. Not that he is ashamed of it, but he doesn't like being set apart from the others. Sure, he knows a lot of Yiddish expressions. His grandparents still speak it sometimes. Mostly he knows the curses. There are a lot of curses. Sometimes he'll recite a curse in Yiddish to his younger brother, but then he feels bad and tells him it was actually a compliment. The one that Josie just said about the fields of intestines is one of his grandmother's favorites. If he told her a girl said it in class she'd be horrified.

Katy Parker scans the crowd at the fire drill. She knows Josie and Megan are in Ms. Connors's class now. Katy has world religions next period, and since she's usually the first person there, she knows everyone who is in the previous period. Ms. Connors is easy to spot because she is one of the tallest female teachers in the school. Katy makes her way over and stands a few feet away until Josie comes to get her. Sometimes being found is easier than finding.

"C'mon, Sara," Amelia says, pulling her cousin into the empty courtyard of the cafeteria. "You owe me."

Sara shakes her head and firmly plants her feet. "What do I owe you for?"

"I'm sure you owe me for something. Why won't you do it?"

"It's not worth getting caught."

"It is to me. What if I promise I'll leave the money for whatever we take?"

Sara narrows her eyes.

Amelia grabs Sara's hand. "C'mon."

By a combination of pushing and dragging, Amelia gets Sara to accompany her into the cafeteria. From one of the tables, Amelia picks up a plastic garbage bag that had housed someone's oversized lunch. She hands it to Sara. Once at the freezer, Amelia needs only ten seconds to expertly jiggle the lock open with her school ID card. She grabs the ice cream sandwiches with both hands and thrusts them at Sara before reaching in a second time. Just then they hear footsteps running through the cafeteria. Amelia hurriedly closes the freezer door and hears the lock click back into place. She motions for Sara to hide behind the counter but finally has to grab her and push her to the floor.

Peeking over the rim, Amelia sees the four girls arrive at the freezer door. She feels the anger rise inside her. This is her gig, no one else's. To Sara's horror, Amelia pops up and says something to the girls about gluttony. Sara has no choice but to stand up too. Her hands are freezing from gripping the sandwiches. When Megan asks her for some ice cream, she really wants to answer her. She always liked Megan and her friends. She didn't think Josie was that great in the fall musical, but she liked how she was fearless on the stage. But Sara doesn't respond to Megan's question. In fact, she won't say more than five words at a time to anyone other than Amelia for another three weeks. Not until her father comes into her room, sits down on her bed, and begins to cry. After that, there'll be no shutting her up.

*   *   *

Zoey's eyes well up with tears when she sees Sara so utterly unable to answer Megan's question. A second ago this whole thing was hysterical, but now Zoey remembers the time in fourth grade when a group of girls surrounded her on the playground and taunted her because she wouldn't answer their questions. *What time is it, Zoey? What's your middle name? What color is your underwear?* Now she can feel the tears coming and is pretty sure her friends assume they are tears of laughter. Zoey has always felt nothing but loathing for that little pale child who couldn't stand up for herself on the playground. But now, this very instant, that hate is replaced with a new forgiveness. Zoey has Sara to thank for that. She never will, though, because she's just not the type. But at graduation, Zoey will clap extra loudly when Sara goes up to receive her diploma.

Grant Brawner arrives back in school just in time to hear the bell ring to end sixth period. He grabs his books from his locker and makes his way to his U.S. government class. He can't stop thinking about Bobby at the maternity ward. One minute he looked like he was about to pass out, the next he was totally in control and helping Sherri get comfortable. Grant stayed while Bobby called Sherri's parents and the couple in Miami who were going to adopt the baby. Bobby told them Sherri had gone into labor early and they should get up here. It struck Grant as the most mature conversation he had ever heard a fellow teenager hold. He felt bad for not having been nicer to Bobby. If only Bobby weren't such a dweeb. He vowed from now on he'd be nicer to people. He gets a whiff of BO as he hurries down the hall and realizes with disgust that it's him. Bobby had him going so crazy that now he smells like a locker room.

Grant is so wrapped up in his thoughts that he doesn't notice he bumps into someone until his books go flying. Of all people, it's that girl Josie who's always following him. He's so out of it he doesn't even know if he apologized. Heck, he figures it probably made her day no matter what he said or didn't say.

During the five minutes before seventh period, the guidance office sees more traffic than it has all year. One by one the students file in, heads down, and drop off their group therapy forms. Rob Taylor isn't afraid that someone will see him there because the form isn't for himself, it's for his sister, Josie. His wounded heart is too fresh for him to realize that it might help him to talk with others who have been through the same thing. And he fully intends to change Anne's mind. But when his teacher handed out the brochures last period he was struck by how well Josie might benefit from one of the groups. He rereads the description one more time before laying his form in the basket on top of the others.

Self-Esteem

Our level of self-esteem affects virtually everything we think, say, and do. It affects how we see the world and our place in it. It affects how others in the world see and treat us. It affects the choices we make — choices about what we will do with our lives and with whom we will be involved. It affects our ability to both give and receive love. And, it affects our ability to take action to change things that need to be changed. Accepting who we are helps us develop a healthy self-esteem and can make a huge impact on how we live our lives. A person with a healthy self-esteem is aware of her potential, knows the many facets that make her unique, and values and respects herself. More importantly, however, he or she knows that her imperfections or inadequacies are not inherently bad, and they do not become overwhelming to the point that they completely define her value as a person. He or she knows that no one's perfect — it's human to have limitations and make mistakes.

Rob hopes he isn't overstepping his bounds. But Josie always seems to know what's best for *him*, so maybe it works both ways. And if she's mad, he doesn't have to tell her that he's the one who signed her up.

* * *

Anne Derkin watches from around the corner as Rob hurries out of the guidance office, his eyes straight ahead. Breaking up with him was the hardest thing she ever had to do. Her friends didn't know what to say when she told them. Nobody understands her reasons. Sherri Haugen would understand. But she's at a hospital now giving birth to a baby she never wanted and whom she's going to hand over to strangers. Anne and Sherri were supposed to go to the University of Virginia together, but Sherri never got her application out. Now Anne is going alone. No one in Anne's family had ever even thought about going to college. She won't let anything derail her plans. Not even love. At least Rob is getting help from the guidance office. That makes her feel a little better.

By the time I get to the auditorium my heart is still beating fast from my run-in with Grant. At first I can't find Megan. Usually there are only twelve people in my drama class, but a lot of other people showed up for the audition. My hope is that they only did it to get out of their last class of the day and don't really care about being in the play. Hopefully they'll all be really bad. I finally sight Megan warming up on stage. I can hear her running through the vowel sounds in one long *aaeeiioouu*. I scramble up onto the stage and tell her about my encounter.

"So then what happened?" she asks.

"You mean after Grant said my name and the world became a little bit brighter?"

"Yeah," she says dryly. "After that."

"He walked away."

Mr. Polansky instructs us to start our deep breathing exercises.

In between breaths, Megan asks, "Have you ever had a real conversation with Grant? I've heard he isn't the nicest guy in the world."

I breathe in through the nose, out through the mouth. "He was very nice when he bumped into me."

Megan shrugs. The stage quickly fills up and I recognize most of the people from *The King and I*. Megan isn't the only one wearing clothes that are a bit more *Romeo and Juliet* than twenty-first-century Florida. Two senior girls that I've never seen before at any of the drama activities hurry onto the stage. Mr. Polansky gives them a big smile.

Megan leans close and whispers, "Those girls used to be in all the plays before we got here."

My stomach knots up. I hadn't counted on fresh competition. Don't they know how important this is to me?

"Okay, people," Mr. Polansky says, stroking his new goatee. "We're going to do a quick exercise before we start the auditions. This is what I want you to do. For the next five minutes you're going to silently act out the full range of emotions. You will need to dig deep inside yourselves to pull out the proper memory or evoke the proper event. Don't worry about what anyone else is doing. Ready? Anger!"

He does this during our regular drama class, so I'm used to it. I barely have enough time to narrow my eyes and look mad when he calls out, "Fear!"

That one's easy. I picture the plane/satellite/tree/roof falling on me, and then cover my head with my arms and duck.

"Love!"

I straighten up and let my features go soft and moony. I picture me and Grant slow-dancing at the prom and almost lift up my arms for real. I glance over at Brad White and Jennifer Bloom, who think they're very special because they have the same first names as another infinitely more famous acting couple. Their shining eyes reflect a longing that I've seen only in the movies. Instead of people, they are two magnets drawn together. I'm not the only one looking at them. Suddenly Brad moves closer to Jennifer and they start making out. Right there on the stage! Mr. Polansky gapes with the rest of us. Then he hurries toward the stage and starts clapping. For a minute I think he's actually applauding them until I realize he's trying to get them to stop.

Megan says loudly, "This is better than cable!"

Brad and Jennifer finally pull apart and seem surprised to find everyone staring at them. Maybe that's what love is all about. It makes the rest of the world go away.

Jennifer's cheeks are bright red.

"Um, sorry," Brad says.

Mr. Polansky clears his throat and we face front again. "Remember people, this is just an exercise! Okay, now show me sadness."

I immediately picture how I would feel if I had failed my driver's test this morning. My face falls, my shoulders slump, and I stare down at the floor. Except now I feel stupid for feeling sad about that when there are so many real things in the world to be sad about. My grandmother once told me that being self-centered is part of being a teenager. She says everything "looms larger" at my age. Well, I'm ready for it to loom smaller already.

"All right," Mr. Polansky says. "Now instead of having you audition for specific roles like in the fall, I'm going to have all the boys read for Romeo and all the girls for Juliet. I'll decide which role would suit you best."

Is he serious? I whip my head around to look at everyone else. No one else seems fazed by this announcement. Now my agreement with Megan never to try out for the same part won't mean anything. Mr. Polansky directs us to line up backstage, where we'll be called up one by one. I'm so flustered that I can't move at first. The thought of someone who only wanted to try out for the nurse or Lady Montague winding up as Juliet is too awful to contemplate. My stomach tightens up.

"Josie," Mr. Polansky says, startling me out of my daze. "Since you're still onstage, why don't you go first?"

I turn full circle and see that I am, in fact, the only person left onstage. I catch sight of Megan standing next to the curtain at stage right. She motions me forward with a big smile. Sure, she can smile, because she doesn't really care about this play. At least by going first I won't have anyone else's performance to live up to. I slowly move to the front of the stage and Mr. Polansky reaches up and hands me a playbook. I take a deep breath and wait until he sits down in the front row. He nods at me and I imagine myself as Juliet, standing on her balcony, peering out at her only love.

"'Tis but thy name that is my enemy; thou art thyself, though not a Montague." Oh my god am I doing okay? "What's Montague? It is nor hand, nor foot, nor arm, nor face, nor any other part —" Are those two senior girls watching me? "Belonging to a man. O, be some other name! What's in a name? That which we call a rose by any other name would smell as sweet —" Ilostmyplacewhatsthenextlineohright! "So Romeo would, were he not Romeo call'd, retain that dear perfection which he owes —" Did I pause too long? Am I talking too fast? "Without that title. Romeo, doff thy name, and for that name which is no part of thee take all myself." Whew!

When I finish I let my hand with the playbook in it fall to my side. Applause from backstage reaches me as Mr. Polansky scribbles some notes on his clipboard.

"Thank you, Josie," he says, resting his clipboard on his knee. "That was very nice. You can come sit down here now."

I nod, but can't seem to make my feet obey. I honestly don't want to get off the stage, but Mr. Polansky is already waving the next girl up. I've never been that nervous before. What's wrong with me? I turn around to see one of the two seniors quickly approaching. She's tall and blond and her skin is almost translucent. She holds out her hand and I place the playbook in it with a weak smile. I walk down the short flight of steps at the side of the stage as slowly as I dare. By the time I choose a seat a few rows behind Mr. Polansky, the girl is already beginning her speech. My spirits sink as I listen. She is really good. The bright stage lights hit her face in such a way that she seems almost lit up from inside. I wonder if I looked anything like that up there. After the girl finishes and the applause stops, Megan steps forward. She takes the playbill from the girl and looks uneasily at Mr. Polansky. I know she hasn't rehearsed much. She reads through the piece a bit halfheartedly. I muster a big smile to urge her on, but she doesn't really get into it. She looks at her feet as Mr. Polansky takes his notes.

Just as he puts his pen down, Mrs. Lombardo from the school office enters from the side door. I don't think I've ever seen her outside of the office before. She seems taller in the real world. She whispers something to Mr. Polansky, who then turns around to me. To me!

"Josie," he says. "You're wanted in the office."

"Don't worry, nothing's wrong," Mrs. Lombardo says, backing up toward the door.

"What's going on?" Megan asks, hurrying down from the stage.

I shake my head. "I have no idea. Maybe my mother forgot to sign the absence note from this morning?" Maybe Mrs. G saw me passing my physics homework to Jeff Grand. Or maybe I'm being honored for being a leaper? I tell Megan not to worry, that I'll see her at Katy's for the scavenger hunt. I run to catch up with Mrs. Lombardo, who is holding the door open for me.

"So, what's going on?"

"Your mother called to say she's on her way over."

"Why? Is something wrong?"

"Nothing's wrong, I promise. Say, how did your driver's test go this morning? I assume you passed. The students who fail usually don't come back in for the day."

"Yes, I passed." Did the DMV call my mother to say they made a mistake? I knew it was too good to be true! If I have to take my test over maybe I can get a better picture taken. Mrs. Lombardo is being annoyingly cryptic. We reach the office and she takes her usual seat behind the desk. She gestures for me to sit on the bench against the wall.

"Your mom should be here in a minute," she says, shuffling through one of the piles of paper that didn't seem to have gotten any smaller since this morning. "So I can also assume you and your friend straightened out the note situation this morning?"

I scoot down the bench to see her better. "What do you mean?"

"I'm sorry I read it, I didn't mean to."

"Read what?"

"The note you gave me."

Why is she apologizing for reading my absence note? I feel like I'm in one of those dreams where two people are talking but the conversation doesn't make any sense.

"I have to go into a staff meeting now," Mrs. Lombardo says, picking up a few folders from her desk. She pushes herself up and heads through the back door. "You'll have to work this out between yourselves."

"Wait!" I call after her. "Work *what* out? Between *who*?" The door swings shut and I'm alone for about two seconds before my mother walks in, carrying a big white bakery box.

"Hi, sweetheart," she says with a big smile. "I was in the neighborhood so I thought I'd drop these off for you to hand out to your class. You know, for your birthday and because you passed your driver's test."

I stare at her.

"You okay?" she asks.

I put my hands on my hips and firmly plant my feet. "No, I am not ok. I've just been pulled out of play tryouts where I had to be the first to audition and everyone's trying out for the same parts, I just had a very bizarre conversation with the school secretary, Megan may be throwing up her cucumber sandwiches, I've broken five of the seven deadly sins in as many hours, a demon may be inside a girl in my world religions class, Grant Brawner called me by name, my license photo looks like a dead fish, I have to drive my friends all over town in two hours when I've never even driven without Dad before, none of my birthday wishes have come true yet, and now you're here with muffins like I'm in second grade? So, no, I am not okay."

The taken-aback look on my mom's face clearly says not only am I not okay, I may actually be insane. She places the box gently on the counter and tentatively reaches out and pats me on the head like I'm a little girl.

"Into every life a little rain must fall," she says in the soothing voice she used to read me to sleep with when I was little. "I know you're not in second grade, but everyone likes muffins, and like I said, I was in the neighborhood. I made more than necessary for the luncheon I catered today. I didn't mean to upset you."

I glance up at the clock on the office wall. There's only a few minutes left in the period and I don't want to miss any more of the auditions. Now, of course, I feel bad because she was just trying to do something nice and I lashed out. Maybe this is why she doesn't usually ask me what's wrong.

"No, it's not you," I tell her, picking up the box. "This was very nice. I'm sure everyone will love them."

I balance the box on my hip while I open the door, but Mom doesn't move to follow me out.

"One more thing," she says. "When your father dropped you off after the test, did he say where he was going this afternoon?"

"No. Why?"

She shakes her head and shrugs a bit. "I picked up a strange phone message for him, but I can't reach him on his cell."

"Who called?"

"The woman said she was calling from City Hall and wanted your father to call her back. It was all very vague."

I try to recall if he said anything about where he was going, but I don't think he did. He *had* been acting a little strange, with all that talk about dreams, but he didn't mention anything about City Hall.

"Is City Hall where the jail is?" I joke. "Maybe Dad's secret life has caught up with him."

Her head tilts. "What secret life?"

"Haven't you noticed he's been sort of secretive for the last two weeks? He's not around the house when we get home from school anymore, either."

Mom shakes her head. "I didn't know that. I've been working so much."

"He's probably just bored because he doesn't have a job, so he's out more."

She nods. "Probably."

I glance at the office clock again and she gets the hint. She gives me a squeeze on the arm and says she'll see me for dinner. That's my mom. Not even asking where I'm going to be after school. Sometimes I think she wants to ask, like it's on the tip of her tongue, but she almost never does.

I'm about to push open the auditorium door when I decide that

I don't actually want to hear any more of the auditions after all. If pressed, I wouldn't be able to explain why. I leave the box of muffins next to the door and take the closest stairs two at a time. Mr. Simon has a free period now and the photography room is empty. He never locks the darkroom so I shouldn't have any trouble picking up my photo from this morning. I turn the knob and start to push the door open when I hear, "Hey, don't you see the light on?" I quickly look up and see that the red light above the door is indeed lit, indicating someone is using the darkroom. But by this time some light has already been let in. Any damage has already been done.

"Sorry 'bout that," I say, and walk the rest of the way in. To my surprise Greg Adler is standing over one of the photo trays, tongs in hand. "What are you doing? Extra credit?"

Greg just looks at me. "Something like that. What are you doing here?"

I point up at the clothesline. "I came for my picture. It's hanging right over your head."

He reaches up and pulls off the photo, handing it to me. There are a couple of streaks over Katy's and Zoey's faces from where the chemicals dripped, but other than that it looks as good as I remember it.

"Thanks," I say, turning to leave. "Sorry I ruined your picture."

"It's okay," he mumbles. "I can make another one."

The dismissal bell rang while I was in the darkroom, so I no longer have the halls to myself. It can't have been more than five minutes since I left the box by the auditorium door, but when I pick it up it's a lot lighter than I remember. I flip the top open and find only crumbs and a pink birthday candle. After carefully tucking the candle into one of my pants pockets, I toss the box into a nearby trash bin. I feel a twinge of guilt that I let the muffins get stolen after Mom went to all that trouble. I'll have to double-check to see if carelessness is one of the seven deadlies.

Luckily by this time Mr. Polansky is calling up the boys. I take a seat in the last row and try to decide who would make the cutest Romeo. The boys are lucky. There are a lot of good boy parts in the play. Finally everyone has had a turn, and Mr. Polansky announces that the results will be up on the school Web site by midnight. I hurry down to the front to grab my bookbag and Megan joins me.

"So why did Mrs. Lombardo come get you?" Megan asks. We head out to wait for her mother in front of the school.

"My mother came and dropped off a box of muffins for my birthday."

"Like you were in second grade?"

"That's what I said!"

"But it was still nice."

"Yeah, it was. But someone stole them from outside the auditorium door."

"That sucks."

"I hope whoever ate them enjoyed them."

"I don't," Megan says matter-of-factly.

"Yeah, me neither." We sit down on the front steps to wait. After a minute I ask, "So how were the other girls?"

Megan pauses. "They were okay. It's hard to tell, you know, just from that short piece. But don't worry, you were one of the best ones."

I manage a small smile. Some people think Megan is self-absorbed, but I think she's a good friend.

"But," she adds, "there *are* good roles besides Juliet, you know."

"Definitely!" I say with more enthusiasm than I actually feel. But I don't want to let Megan down. The best she can hope for from her performance is probably Juliet's mother, Lady Capulet.

Megan's mother pulls up, and on the way to Katy's house Megan tells her it's my birthday today.

"Yes, I knew that," she says. "I spoke to Josie's mother this morning."

"You did?" I knew my mom had threatened to call her about Megan not eating anything, but I never thought she'd really do it.

"Yes," Megan's mom says. "We had a nice conversation."

She doesn't say anything more, so neither do I. Megan is oblivious to us, softly singing to herself, "Tale as old as time, song as old as rhyme, Beauty and the Beast." She really has a beautiful voice. It's a good thing she hadn't tried out for Anna last fall or I never would have gotten the part.

Jennifer Bloom waits for Mr. Polansky to call out the next emotion. Right now they are in the middle of "fear," and she's picturing herself dying in her bed alone because she heard Brad is going to break up with her after auditions today. She heard this from a friend who heard it from her sister who heard it from Brad's brother who heard Brad talking on the phone. She can't imagine why he would do it. They have been happily together since middle school. They won "Best Couple" in their eighth-grade year-book. Maybe he's tired of her. Maybe he wants someone who looks more exotic and curvy, like Megan over there.

Brad White watches Jennifer out of the corner of his eye. Her face is pale and haunted-looking. He wonders what she is imagining. Fear is an easy emotion for him to do. He just pictures Jennifer breaking up with him be-fore he finally has persuaded her to have sex, and then he has to start all over with another girl. Not that he doesn't love Jennifer — he very much does. But still, it's been a long time of just kissing and touching.

Mr. Polansky calls out "Love," and Jennifer can't help but turn toward Brad. All of her memories of him holding her in his arms, whispering how beautiful she is, the time he won her the huge stuffed turtle at the county fair, all of it shows on her face and she feels like she's melting.

Brad immediately turns to Jennifer when he hears that "love" is the next emotion. He thinks of the times she allowed his hands to wander, the times she made him chocolate chip cookies with M&M's hidden inside, the time she cheered him on when he tossed a ring onto a Coke bottle and won her a huge stuffed turtle. The next thing he knows they are kiss-ing, right there on the stage, in front of everyone.

* * *

Jennifer is the first to pull away when she hears Mr. Polansky clapping at them. She has never loved Brad more or been surer that he loves her too. The grapevine must have been wrong. He would never break up with her.

Jennifer is right, Brad will never break up with her. But a year from now, Jennifer will break up with him when she finds him in the second-floor janitor's closet with a freshman girl named Candy. Jennifer will leave school for the day without telling the office. She will go straight home to cut Brad's head out of four years of photographs.

Mr. Polansky holds his breath while Josie performs. He's glad she wound up going first so that each performance will have to measure up to hers. It will help him judge better. He can tell she's upset by the way he structured the audition, but she still gives a fine performance. She really does come alive up there. He wishes he could focus only on what would be best for the play itself, without having to worry about the kids' feelings on top of it. But he can't. He feels like it's part of his job to help shape them like they are balls of clay. His decisions have the power to affect the rest of their lives. He has to tread carefully.

After Josie leaves with Mrs. Lombardo, Megan watches the rest of the auditions. She can't imagine how Mr. Polansky will make his choice between Josie and the two senior girls. She leans forward and tries to peer over his shoulder to read his notes, but he's covering them with his arm. Last fall Mr. Polansky had told her that her singing voice was the strongest in the play and that she should have auditioned for Anna. Maybe that's why he organized it differently this year, so people couldn't decide what roles to try for. But she and Josie had made a deal, and Josie wants Juliet more than her. It's almost like Josie *needs* it with a kind of need that scares Megan a little, and she's not easily scared. With her peasant blouse on, Megan had really felt like Juliet. For about one minute she had thought about just going for it. But she couldn't. Somewhere deep inside, Megan knows this won't be the last time she'll have to make the choice.

Josie's mom walks slowly down the school steps toward her station wagon. When Josie turned thirteen, her mom had made a conscious decision to be a more hands-off type of mother than her own was. That way, she figured Josie wouldn't resent her the way she had resented her own mother. She can still hear her mother's voice ringing in her ears. *A little lipstick wouldn't kill you; you want a boyfriend someday, don't you? Where are you going? Did you do all your homework? I don't want you hanging out with that girl. Those pants are too tight for you.* And on and on and on. By the time she was grown up and out of the house her mother no longer judged or criticized her every move. But the damage had been done. She figures if she leaves Josie alone, they can be friends after the teen years are over. One of the women at the catering hall keeps tabs on her daughter by reading her daughter's diary every day after she leaves for school. Josie's mom thinks that's a terrible invasion of privacy. Back in the office, it was all she could do not to laugh when Josie rattled off her laundry list of teenage woes. She almost said, "Snap out of it. You won't even remember half this stuff in a year." But she didn't want to seem unfeeling, especially not today. She can't help it if once every four years she goes overboard to make sure Josie's Leap Day birthday is special. On this one day she can forget Josie is growing up and changing every day, right under her nose.

Mrs. Lombardo hurries out of her staff meeting to use the copier in the library because the one in the office is broken again. On her way she sees a big white box sitting on the floor by the auditorium doors. Intrigued, she bends down, creaking as she goes, and lifts the top. *Muffins! Why would someone leave a perfectly good box of what appear to be homemade muffins in the middle of the hall? A trash can is not so much as two feet away! Kids are so lazy.* She picks up the box and is about to toss it when she suddenly changes direction and heads back into her meeting. The office staff gobbles down the muffins, and one of them points to a candle on the bottom of the box. Mrs. Lombardo peeks in and suddenly is not so confident that the box was intended as garbage. She excuses herself again and returns it to the exact spot she took it from. She hurries to the office without looking back. The photocopies can wait.

Greg Adler is rendered speechless when Josie Taylor, of all people, walks into the darkroom. *Darn Mr. Simon and his no-lock-on-the-door policy!* Greg quickly turns toward her so that his body blocks his tray. He can only hope that in the inky darkness she won't be able to see that he had used her negative to develop another copy of her photo with Zoey in it. He hadn't even known he was going to do it until a few minutes ago. He had gotten permission to use Mr. Simon's empty room to practice his bar mitzvah material, since he had study hall this period anyway. And then he went into the darkroom to check on his own picture and the next thing he knew, he couldn't stop staring at Zoey and her stupid hot dog.

Josie finally leaves and Greg breathes a sigh of relief. He didn't want to tell her that she hadn't ruined his picture, because he was afraid she would want to see it. He swishes it around in the solution for another minute and then carefully lifts it out. Since he can't very well hang it to dry, he waves it in the air for a few minutes and then sticks it between the pages of his notebook. When he gets home he'll find that most of the photo is stuck to the notebook paper except for the picnic table, the hot dog, and Zoey's arm.

"It's about time you guys got here," Zoey says, tapping her watch. "Only three more minutes to go."

Katy swings around in her desk chair to face us. The school Web site is up on her computer. "So how did the audition go?"

"Pretty good, I guess," I tell her, not wanting to talk about it.

"Don't listen to her," Megan says. "Josie was great."

"So were you," I reply, even though we both know she wasn't.

"When do you find out?" Katy asks, keeping one eye on her computer screen. She hits the refresh button, but it's still not there yet.

"Tonight. By midnight."

I pull out the picture of Zoey and Katy, and while they are *ooh*ing and *ahh*ing at it, I take my gift from Niki out of my bag and climb onto Katy's bed. Using my new car key, I slit open the tape on the box. The card on top reads, "To my favorite leapmate on our fourth birthday, just a little something I thought you could use to even things out." *To even things out?* What does that mean? I dig through a layer of squishy packing peanuts and pull out a small purple tube. How strange. I turn it over in my hand until I find the even-smaller label.

Breast Boost

Rub this lavender-scented lotion onto your breasts each night before bed to achieve fullness and growth.
Guaranteed!

I immediately thrust the tube back in the box, hoping no one saw it. Luckily they are still watching the screen. I should be grateful I didn't open the box in the car when Dad gave it to me. As high as my embarrassment threshold is, it ain't high enough for that.

"It's up!" Zoey squeals. "Quick, turn on the printer."

I push the small box into the bottom of my bookbag and join them by the desk. At least now I know what I'll be doing before bed tonight.

The screen blinks the words: "The Orlando High Sophomore Scavenger Hunt," in our school colors, purple on a bright yellow background. I am suddenly excited to do this. There aren't too many good things about being a sophomore, but the scavenger hunt is one of them. Plus, it will take my mind off the play. It's nice to have a much-needed break from focusing on myself. As we wait for the list to print, Katy reads the rules out loud.

1. Teams may consist of no more than four members, all of the same sex. All must be sophomores.

2. Team members must stay within fifty feet of each other at all times.

3. No help allowed from parents, siblings, or the general public except in a driving capacity.

4. You are not allowed to tell people what you are doing so that they'll give you stuff.

5. No money shall be spent with the exception of gas.

6. Judging will begin at 6 P.M. sharp at Jenny Waxner's house. Any latecomers will be disqualified. In case of a tie, the victory will go to whichever team completed the hunt first.

7. Bonus points will be given for creativity and especially hard-to-find items.

Prizes:

First place: Dinner with one of the Backstreet Boys/*NSYNC/ O-Town when he is in Orlando, compliments of Jenny's father's public relations company.

Second place: Your choice of free spa treatments at the Orlando Day Spa, compliments of Jenny's mother's frequent guest plan, OR floor seats at the next Orlando Magic game.

Third through tenth place: Free dinner at Sizzler, compliments of Sizzler on 4th and Willow.

"Aren't all those boy band guys old and married now?" Zoey asks. "Why would we want to have dinner with them?"

"Maybe we'd get to be on MTV," Megan says, pulling the pages out of the printer. "But if we don't get organized and get moving, we won't even get the free dinner at Sizzler." She hands the list to Katy, the natural choice to lead us.

"Okay," Katy says, whipping out a red pen. "I'll be the list-keeper. I'll tell us what we still need and cross off the items we've found. Josie is the driver. Zoey, you'll be the time-keeper. Every ten minutes you'll update us on how much longer until we have to get to Jenny's."

"What do I do?" Megan asks. "Stand here and look pretty?"

Katy taps her pen against the desk in thought. "You'll be the motivator. You'll keep us moving. I'll read the list now, and everyone jump in if you know where we can find something."

"As the motivator," Megan says, "I think we should just get going."

"If we spend five minutes now, we'll save ourselves a lot of extra running-around time."

"Fine. Just tell us what's on the list."

"Okay. Each item has a point value, with the hardest-to-find items having the most points. To start with, we need something with four legs."

"Right here," I say, plucking Katy's stuffed Garfield from her pillow.

"Good," Katy said, crossing that item off the list with a flourish. "There's an old duffle bag from camp in my closet. Let's put everything in there."

I pull out the dusty green duffle and stick Garfield inside.

"Next is something that's been dead for over a year. Hmm. That's pretty weird."

"There's a dead bee that's been stuck in the screen of my bedroom window since last summer," Zoey offers.

"I have a better idea," Megan announces. "Fang."

"My cat?" Zoey asks, confused. Then, "Oh no, you mean his ashes?"

"It's perfect!"

Zoey looks at me for support. "It *is* creative," I admit. "We may need those bonus points in the end."

"Fang would want to help," Katy says. "He was that kind of cat."

Zoey gives a long sigh and says, "All right. But I'm not just throwing his tin in that duffle. Someone has to hold it at all times."

"Fine," Katy says, and crosses it off the list.

Zoey looks at her watch. "An hour and fifty minutes."

"Next are a bunch of things we can find right here. Something three different shades of white — hey, that could be you, Zoey!"

"Very funny," Zoey says.

Katy continues. "Something hot, something cold, something

that uses electricity, a photograph of two people kissing, letterhead from a university, a model of a spaceship, a half-eaten burrito, the picture of President George W. Bush pardoning the Thanksgiving turkey in 2001, two identical organic (non-manmade) things, a menu from Donald's Hot Dog Hut at Magic Kingdom, and a weekly newspaper from the town of Celebration."

"Gee, is that all?" Megan asks sarcastically. "How are we supposed to do all that in less than two hours?"

"There are bonus items too," Katy says, turning the page. "An extra twenty points if we bring in either an undergarment from a teacher at Orlando High, a copy of the *Kama Sutra,* or a bottle of Gee Your Hair Smells Terrific shampoo. Remember, we're not allowed to buy anything from a store."

"What's the *Kama Sutra?*" I ask. "And didn't they stop making that shampoo when we were like, six?"

"The *Kama Sutra* is an ancient sex manual," Zoey explains. "That will be easy to get."

"How will that be easy?" Katy asks.

Zoey grins. "My brother has it under his bed."

"Your brother is being very helpful today," Megan says, nodding appreciatively.

"What do you mean?" I ask. I've never heard of Dennis being anything but a pain in the butt.

"Oh, nothing," Megan says quickly. "Just that now we'll get all those bonus points."

"Tick tick tick," Zoey says loudly.

Katy scrambles into gear. She tells Zoey and Megan to go next door for Fang's ashes and the sex book, and sends me downstairs while she looks up the George Bush picture online. In the kitchen, I grab a zip-lock bag and mix salt, flour, and sugar. Voilà! Three different shades of white. Something is nagging at the back of my brain, but I can't think what it is. Anyway, I need to focus right now. A can of Coke from the fridge wrapped in layers of tin foil will have to do as the something cold. My last item to find is the flashlight Katy's dad keeps in the garage. She figures when you turn it on, that will be the something hot. Katy's very smart that way. I run upstairs to dump my items in the duffle.

"Throw in my clock radio too," Katy instructs me, pounding away on her keyboard. "For something that uses electricity."

I unplug the clock and stick it next to the stuffed Garfield so it won't get banged around too much. Megan and Zoey still aren't back yet. I finally have a chance to talk to Katy alone.

"You've got to tell me now, about the note. You're killing me here."

Katy stops typing and slowly turns in her seat. Just then Megan and Zoey run breathlessly into the room, and Katy quickly turns back to her computer. Crap. The moment has passed. Zoey sits down on the bed and cradles the purple tin of ashes in her arms.

"There are some bizarre pictures in this book," Megan says, flipping through the well-worn paperback. She turns the book upside down. "I didn't think the body could move that way."

"Later, okay?" Katy says, snatching the book from Megan's hands. She retrieves the Bush/turkey picture from the printer, sticks it between the pages of the book, and tosses the book in the ever-expanding bag.

"What now?" Zoey asks.

Katy looks down at her list. "I can use my mother's Disney passes to get us into the park for the menu, and then from there we can go to Celebration for the newspaper. The other little stuff we can try to find on the way."

"Maybe your mother can just get us the menu," Megan suggests. "Then we can spend more time on the rest."

Katy shakes her head. "No parental involvement. It's in the rules."

"Do you always have to follow the rules?" Zoey asks, already knowing Katy won't budge.

And then it hits me. "Uh-oh," I say, sinking to the bed. "I don't have the car. Rob drove it home after school while we were at the audition."

Three mouths fall open. Katy hands me the phone. "Call Rob and see if he's home."

My mother answers and tells me Rob is out doing Dart Wars, which I had forgotten all about.

Zoey whispers, "Ask her if you can borrow her car."

I shake my head and hang up. "She's leaving to pick up my dad's parents for dinner."

"How about your dad then?" Katy asks.

"Not there either," I say. He's apparently still among the missing.

"Then we'll take my mother's minivan," Katy announces. "It's in the garage, and plus, the extra room will be helpful once we have all the stuff with us."

"That thing is huge!" I argue. "How am I supposed to drive it?"

Megan pats me on the back. "You'll do fine."

"I'm not taking it without asking your mother first." I bet she'll say no and I'll get out of it. Who would want their teenage daughter's friend to drive their car around town on the very first day she has her license?

"Fine," Katy says, dialing her mother's work number. "But I'm telling you she won't mind." She presses the speakerphone button so we can all hear.

"Rides and Attractions," the young woman on the other end says perkily. You have to be perky to work at Disney. It's a requirement.

Katy asks for her mother.

"She had to go out to the site," the woman replies. "I'll connect you."

A few seconds later Katy's mother's voice comes on. "Small World," she says, sounding much more stressed than perky. In the background we can hear that ever-present recording, "There is just one moon and one golden sun, and a smile means friendship to everyone. . . ."

"Mom, it's Katy."

"Hi, honey," she says hurriedly. "Can't talk long. Some kid leaned over the boat and drank the water. Now he's running around the displays yelling, 'I am the Lizard King.' His mother says he saw it on a *Simpsons* episode."

Megan covers her mouth to keep from laughing.

"Stop him," Katy's mom yells in the background. "He's knocking over the dolls! Do you know how much those things cost to repair?" Then, "Katy, can I call you back?"

"I just need to know if we can borrow your minivan. Josie has her license now and we have the scavenger hunt today."

"Fine. The keys are hanging in the laundry room. Uh-oh, the kid is throwing up now. Gotta go." The phone clicks off and Katy hangs up.

"Wow," Zoey says. "Your mom has a really cool job."

"Let's go," Katy says, ignoring my little whimpering noises.

We get the keys and climb into the car. Megan stuffs the duffle in the far back. I examine the dashboard and finally accept the fact that it's not very different from my dad's or the car at the DMV, except that everything is larger and the front of the car slopes down. I twist the key in the ignition and, to my relief, it sputters and dies.

"I guess we'll have to find someone else to drive us," I say, trying to sound sad.

"Try again," Katy urges. "It just needs to warm up. She doesn't drive it that often."

I turn it again, and this time it purrs to life. Rats. I slowly back out of the garage. I feel like I'm driving a school bus.

"Ninety minutes left," Zoey announces from behind me. "Can you speed up there a little, Grandma?"

"If I get a ticket of any kind," I tell them as we head down the street, "we split it four ways." It is very strange to be riding with my friends without a parent present. I glance in the rearview mirror and see that Zoey has the purple tin on her lap. She and Megan have strapped themselves in. Probably a good idea.

"How are you feeling?" Katy asks. "You're doing an excellent job. Not swaying nearly as much as you usually do."

"I sway?" I turn my head toward her, and a car honks at me for coming too close to the other lane. I swerve back and almost go into the oncoming traffic. Katy holds onto the dashboard for dear life.

"Hey, eyes on the road up there," Megan says, a little shakily.

"Sorry."

We stop at a light, where a mother with a baby carriage crosses in front of us.

"That's ten points!" Zoey says, leaning forward between Katy and me.

Katy looks down at her list. "Huh?"

"No, not in the scavenger hunt! It's something my brother

taught me. If you hit a baby carriage it's ten points, an old man is five points, things like that."

"That's a great game," Katy says. "Your brother needs professional help."

"True," Zoey agrees, leaning back.

"And I don't think Josie needs any more incentive to hit things," Megan whispers.

"I heard that," I tell her, pulling in the front gate of the Magic Kingdom.

Luckily the car has Katy's mother's employee-parking sticker on it, so we pull up to a special toll booth. The woman inside leans out, sees the sticker, and is about to wave us through when she says, "Wait, are you old enough to drive?"

The others giggle and I sigh, pulling my new license out of my pocket and handing it to her. She looks at it and hands it back.

"Sorry," she says. "You look younger."

"I get that a lot."

"Well, don't let it bother you. When you're my age you'll love it when people say you don't look your age." I don't tell her I've heard that a hundred times from everyone older than twenty-one. She presses a button and the orange arm lifts. I drive into the employee-parking lot, where luckily we won't have to wait for a tram.

"Does anyone know where this Donald's Hut place is?" Zoey asks as we pile out and run toward the front entrance.

"It's in Fantasyland," Katy says. She's by far the most Disney-educated of all of us. She hands the ticket-taker the free passes, and he lets us in. We run down Main Street toward Cinderella Castle, which leads straight into Fantasyland.

"Why isn't it called *Cinderella's* Castle?" Megan asks. "You know, as in belonging to Cinderella?"

"No one knows," Katy answers. "But if you call it Cinderella's Castle the people who work here get very upset."

I vow that if I get the Snow White gig, I will let the guests call the castle anything they darn well please. We run through the castle and past the huge carousel. Donald Duck's big head suddenly looms in front of us. The restaurant is one of those outdoor ones where you walk up to a window and order and then pay a cashier on the other side. All of the windows have lines, so we go over to one of the cashiers. Her red and white name tag has a picture of Mickey Mouse and says, BRENDA, and under that, the city she grew up in, ATLANTA, GEORGIA.

"Hello, Brenda," Megan says sweetly. "Do you have a menu we can take with us?"

Brenda shakes her head. "The menu is up there," she replies in an equally sweet, and very Southern, accent and points to the big plastic sign above the food windows.

"But don't you have a paper menu?" Zoey asks. "Or even a plastic one?"

"No, we sure don't. Just that one."

"Are you sure?"

"Yup. Why does everyone keep askin' for a menu today?"

"Other people have asked for menus?" Megan asks.

She nods. "A whole bunch of kids. Around your age. Told 'em all the same thing."

We walk out of the Hut and sit on the bench. "At least no one else can get it either," Megan says. "They led us on a wild goose chase." She points to Donald's big head and giggles. "A wild duck chase."

"Wait, I know," Katy says, taking the list out of her back pocket. "We'll just write down the menu. That should count."

It's those kinds of ideas that make Katy our natural leader.

"Seventy minutes left," Zoey announces as Katy finishes scribbling down the menu. Luckily it only consists of eight items.

We run past the tourists who are beginning to line Main Street for the next parade. I wish we could stay to see who they have doing Snow White. That way I could judge my competition for the summer. I pause for one second in the hopes of catching sight of her, and right as I turn around a little girl with a long brown ponytail races past me at top speed, crying as she goes. She can't be more than eight. A Disney employee is close on her heels, talking into a walkie-talkie. As the employee runs past me my heart suddenly seizes up. It's my *father!* My father in blue polyester slacks, a white shirt, and a red vest that says GUEST RELATIONS HOST in dark blue letters on the back. I blink my eyes in disbelief.

At the same second that I recognize him, he stops and stares at me. By this time my friends have turned around to see what's keeping me. Their jaws drop in unison.

"Dad?" I ask, in a small voice. "What's going on?" The girl runs into a bathroom. The outside is decorated to look like a big tree trunk so it blends in with the scenery.

He looks from me to the bathroom to my friends and back to me again. "I don't have time to explain," he says. "I can't go in there, and it's my job to help that child."

"It is? Since when?" I consider asking Katy to pinch me to make sure I'm not dreaming. On his chest is the same red-and-white plastic tag that Brenda at the Duck Hut had. Except underneath the small Mickey Mouse design his tag says JONATHAN. TAMPA, FLORIDA. Hanging below the tag is a little red ribbon with the words: EARNING MY EARS. I'm trying not to freak out but my heart is racing faster than when I thought Instructor Joe was dead.

"Since today, actually. I'm still officially in training. See the ribbon? I could lose my job if I can't help her. Will you go in there and try to get her out? You have a knack for putting people at ease. Maybe she'll open up to you."

"I do?" I look around me. "I have a knack?"

My friends, still struck mute, nod in agreement.

He nods too. "People are drawn to you. I've seen it your whole life."

I don't know if he said that just to butter me up or not, but a compliment is a compliment. I have so many more questions to ask, but we're in such a hurry and time is clearly of the essence for Dad too. "Where are her parents?"

"Looking for her, I'm sure. I called City Hall and told them I found her."

"You called the *police?*"

Katy chimes in. "There's a building here called City Hall, by the entrance of the park. It's where the guest relations office is located."

Dad nods, and Katy steps back a few feet again.

"So why is she crying?"

Surprisingly, a brief smile crosses his face. "This is right up your alley. She's scared of the ghosts in the Haunted Mansion."

"The ones that get in your car at the end?"

"Yup. Sound familiar?"

"Hey, I didn't cry after the ride!" Just *during* it, but my friends don't need to know that.

"Will you help her?" he pleads.

"All I have to do is explain the ghosts are just holograms, right? Like you told me when I was little?"

He shifts his weight from side to side. "Actually, you can't say that."

"Why not?

"We have to 'preserve the magical guest experience' at all times," he says apologetically. "It's rule number three in the handbook. You'll have to figure something else out. Free cotton candy maybe? Hurry."

I turn to my friends. Zoey glances meaningfully at her watch. "Go ahead," Katy says with a light shove. "We'll wait."

It's not like they have much choice, since I'm the driver.

With one last glance at the stranger who is my father, I hurry into the bathroom. I've never done anything like this before. Why should someone listen to anything I have to say? I know, I'll pretend I'm acting in a play! When I get inside, I find the girl huddled under the counter, wiping her face with some toilet paper.

"Hi," I say to her, cringing a little at how loud it comes across. Megan would love the acoustics in this place! "My name's Josie," I say more softly this time. "I used to be scared of those ghosts too. Maybe I can help."

The little girl sniffles, and I feel her pain, I really do.

"Do you want to go back outside, and we can talk there?"

She shakes her head and doesn't meet my eyes. Okay, so we'll just have to do this here. In a bathroom. "Those ghosts looked like they were having fun, right? They seemed happy. So really, there's nothing to be afraid of."

The girl keeps crying. The collar of her Hello Kitty t-shirt is getting wet. I grab a paper towel and hand it to her. She takes it and lets her hands fall to her side. I don't think I'm doing very well here. Heck, just because Dad has to "preserve the magical guest experience" doesn't mean I have to.

"You know," I say, "it's very possible those ghosts aren't even real. I've heard rumors that they might just be holograms, like in a movie."

The girl shakes her head. "They're real! I know they are!" She swipes at her wet eyes angrily.

"What makes you say that?" Hey, at least she's saying something. That's a good sign.

She sniffles. "One of them . . . spoke to me."

Huh? I didn't see that coming. All I can think to ask is, "What did the ghost say?"

The girl meets my eyes for the first time. For the moment, she has stopped crying. "It was my nana. She said, 'Don't worry, Sloane, I'm here. We'll go home together after the ride.' But now she's not here anymore!"

"So it's not that you were scared of the ghost, it's that your nana isn't around when she said she'd be?"

Sloane nods her head. She wipes at her eyes again, but less angrily. A thin silver bracelet on her wrist catches the light.

"That's a beautiful bracelet."

She looks down at it. "My nana gave it to me for my birthday last year."

"You must have loved her very much."

Sloane nods. "She named me," she says, sitting up a little straighter.

"How come she gave you such an unusual name?"

Sloane thinks for a while and says, "Nana said people with unusual names lead unusual lives." When she says *unusual* it comes out like *anooshal*.

"She sounds like a smart lady."

Sloane doesn't answer. She just stares down at her bracelet. I don't want to lose her so I ask, "What kinds of things did you like to do together?"

Finally she says, "She used to love coming here. She wouldn't go on any of the rides, though. She'd just watch me." Sloane's lips twitch in the first sign of a smile that I've seen.

I move closer to her. "Sloane, do you think it's possible that your nana was telling you that she's always with you, whether you're here in Disney World or at home?"

Sloane tilts her head slightly, looking up at me.

"Maybe it was her way of letting you know she'll always be inside your heart."

Sloane thinks for a few seconds and then nods. Her face brightens.

I smile. "You're a lucky girl to have a nana who loves you so much."

Sloane smiles for real now and reaches for me to help her out from under the counter.

"There's someone outside waiting to give all little girls named Sloane some cotton candy." The words are barely out of my mouth when she runs out of the bathroom. That girl might have a future on the track team.

When I get back out into the bright sunlight, I see Sloane holding my dad's hand, dragging him toward the cotton candy stand like nothing was ever wrong. He turns to look at me over his shoulder. He's beaming. Zoey points frantically at her watch.

I wave goodbye to my dad and Sloane as Megan grabs onto my t-shirt and yanks. We take off in a run down the center of Main Street.

"I'm really sorry I made us lose so much time," I say, huffing.

"Don't worry about it," Katy says. "You were only gone six minutes."

"Really? It felt longer."

"Whatever you said must have worked."

"I guess so. Did my dad say anything to you guys while I was in there?"

The three of them exchange glances. "Not really," Megan says. "Just some stuff about working here always being a dream of his."

"Really? He never mentioned anything like this before." As I say it, I remember our talk on the way to my driver's test. All that stuff about following your dreams. I guess he was just waiting for the right moment to tell me. But the moment found itself, instead.

We hurry through the exit turnstiles and Katy squeezes my arm. "Helping kids seems like a pretty cool job to me."

I smile gratefully. Yeah, it really *is* a pretty cool job. It feels nice to know that after the first few minutes in there, I hadn't been acting anymore.

As we head into the parking lot, four girls I recognize from my gym class run past us. Two of them have big knapsacks on their backs, filled to the brim. Megan says, "What, are they afraid to leave their stuff in the car?"

I can't help being a bit jealous. "It looks like they have a lot of things already."

"Hey, at least they won't find any menus at Donald's Hot Dog Hut," Zoey says.

"You think we should warn them?" Katy asks. We all look at her like she has two heads. "Just kidding," she says. As we approach the car she checks her list. "What are we going to do about the two identical organic things?"

"How about two rocks?" Zoey suggests. "Or leaves?"

We look down at the asphalt. Every pebble we pick up is slightly different.

"I know!" I say loudly, asserting my new feeling of being capable. "We'll get the Davis twins! They're identical and organic!"

"Interesting!" Megan says, her eyes lighting up. "Think of all the bonus points for creativity. I can see us now, introducing videos on MTV, rubbing shoulders with all the famous people . . ."

"But we can't have more people join our team," Katy points out.

"They won't have to join," I say. "They'll just be two more items on the list. We'll make sure they don't help us."

"What if they're on the scavenger hunt too?"

"We won't know unless we try."

She agrees, and we hop in the car and head back out to the main part of town. Megan says she knows where the Davis boys live because they are on her bus route. We pull in front of the house and get out. No one moves more than a foot away from the car.

"Who's gonna ring the bell?" Zoey asks.

"Well," Megan says, "since I'm the motivator, I say Josie goes up there. She knows them the best."

I try to argue. "I don't even know which is which."

"Nobody does," Megan answers, giving me a slight push on the arm.

I guess it's only fair since it was my idea. I take a deep breath and walk up the path. I press the doorbell right away, before I can chicken out. One of the boys opens the door. He has a grape ice pop in his hand and is clearly surprised to see me. He lowers his arm and the ice pop almost touches the sides of his white shorts.

I put on my best smile and say, "Hi, Tom. Er, Tyson. Tom. Tyson?"

"Tom," he says. His eyes dart around, clearly not sure what to make of this visit.

I glance behind me and he follows my gaze. The others are still waiting by the car. They wave. Tom haltingly waves back, ice pop dripping all the while. "This is going to sound strange, but if you and Tyson aren't busy right now, would you mind coming with us on a scavenger hunt? I'll explain on the way. The rules say I can't pay you, but I'll buy you lunch tomorrow at school."

"Sure, we'll do it," Tyson says, coming up behind Tom at the door. Mental note: Tom is wearing white shorts, Tyson's are blue. "We're not busy, right, Tom?"

Tom looks uncertain. "I guess not. I'll go tell Mom." He leaves the doorway, and Tyson and I stand there.

"So, did everything work out with Mrs. Lombardo?" he asks.

"Huh?"

"You know, in photography today. You forgot to hand in your note."

"Oh, right. Well, it got sorted out in the end. I think." Another mental note: Tyson is the one who spoke to me in class today. Tom joins us again, and we head down the driveway. "Don't you guys want to know why we need you?"

"Oh, we know," Tyson says. "Even though we're not playing the game, we saw the list on the Web site. We were wondering if anyone would think of us."

I make the introductions at the car.

Zoey looks Tom over and says, "Are you the frog kid from grammar school?"

Tom nods and stares down at his sneakers.

"I didn't live here then," Zoey says, "but I heard about it."

Tom opens his mouth to say something, then closes it again.

"You guys will have to sit in the way back," Megan says.

"That's fine," Tyson says as Tom scrambles in. "We have older brothers, so we're used to it."

"Hey," Zoey says, passing the tin of ashes to Tyson. "Would you mind hanging on to this? Be careful. It's my cat."

"Uh, okay," Tyson says, holding it at arm's length.

Before she joins them inside, Megan whispers, "Are they allowed to talk to us?"

"Of course they can talk," Katy says. "They just can't help us."

For a second Katy and I are outside the car alone. I whisper to her, "Don't think I'm letting you get away today without telling me what on Earth is in that note."

"Tonight at the lake," she replies, opening the passenger door. "I promise."

Zoey and Megan run across the lawn that connects Zoey's house with Katy's.

"What'll we do if your brother is home?" Megan asks Zoey. "Are you just gonna ask him for the book?"

"He's not home," Zoey says, turning the key in the front door. "He's starting his twenty hours of community service today."

"What did he do this time?"

Zoey pushes open the door, which always sticks. "He set a Port-a-Potty on fire at the county fair last month."

"How'd he get caught?" Megan asks, following Zoey upstairs.

"He always gets caught," Zoey replies. She puts her ear to Dennis's door just to be on the safe side and then pushes it open. As usual, it smells like incense and old socks. She wades through the magazines and dirty clothes and kneels by the bed.

Megan hesitates at the door. A poster of a girl in a bikini is stuck on the ceiling over the bed.

"How come your mother lets him keep that there?" Megan asks.

"Oh, she doesn't come in here. The smell gives her a headache." Zoey reaches under the bed with both arms and sweeps out whatever is within reach. Megan is curious now and carefully steps over to the bed. On the floor are two *Playboys*, a pack of Marlboro Lights, and two bottles of blackberry brandy.

"I know it's here somewhere," Zoey says, reaching under again. This time she pulls out a pair of striped boxer shorts, the book they are looking for, and a locked diary.

"That's weird," Zoey says. "I got this diary when I was in fifth grade. I thought I'd lost it when we moved."

Megan takes it from her and tries to open it. The lock holds tight. "So Dennis stole your diary? What a jerk."

Zoey shakes her head. "No, I never wrote in it. He must be using it."

"We better just take the book, grab Fang's tin, and get back to Katy's," Megan says. The smell in the room is starting to overwhelm her. She picks up the *Kama Sutra* and at the last second scoops up the cigarettes too. They could come in handy tonight.

Zoey pushes everything else back under the bed, including the diary. She knows she could pick the lock if she wanted to, but she's not really that interested in knowing her brother's innermost thoughts. If she had read it, she would have learned that Dennis likes doing the community service more than he likes doing the crime that leads him there. She would have learned that he also likes ancient Roman pottery, puppies but not dogs, and girls with long legs. That he wonders if he has an excessive amount of hair on his knuckles and toes, and that he fears there is no afterlife. But she doesn't pick the lock, she never reads it, and so she will think the bloody razor she finds in the shower is a suicide attempt instead of Dennis's attempt to shave his hairy knuckles. After she tells their parents, Dennis will wind up in therapy because he is too embarrassed to tell his family the truth. At the suggestion of his therapist, he'll begin writing poetry. One of his poems will win a fifty-dollar prize from *Writes of Passage*, a literary magazine for teenagers.

While Josie is checking out the dashboard of Katy's mother's minivan, Katy straps herself into the passenger seat. She then lets her right arm fall to the side of her seat and reaches behind her. Her hand opens to reveal two chewable motion-sickness pills. Zoey silently takes one and passes the other to Megan. As much as they all love Josie, it never hurts to take precautions.

Brenda Mae Brown from Atlanta has been a cashier at Donald's Hot Dog Hut since it opened twelve years ago. Over the last hour six groups of kids have asked her for a menu. Only three of the groups figured out they could write it out themselves. She wonders if she should've told those boys that the red markers they used on their stomachs were permanent ink.

Sloane and her mother are enjoying the Haunted Mansion ride as their car turns a corner on the tracks and faces a long mirror on the darkened wall. Sloane waves at herself in the mirror and then watches with curiosity as a ghostly female figure with a huge grin appears in their car. At first she's scared and starts to reach out for her mother. Then she distinctly hears her grandmother's voice say, "Don't worry, Sloane, I'm here. We'll go home after the ride." What she really heard was the woman in the car in front, trying to get her five-year-old kid to stop crying. "Don't worry, son, I'm here. We'll go home after the ride." Now Sloane is waiting patiently for the Haunted Mansion ride to end. When the metal bar across her lap springs open, she and her mother carefully step onto the moving walkway. Her mother takes her hand and leads her outside.

"Wait, Mommy," Sloane says, pulling back. "We should wait here for Nana."

"What do you mean?"

"Nana said she'd be coming home with us," Sloane explains. "But I don't see her."

Her mother squats down and puts her hands on Sloane's shoulders. "Honey, Nana is in heaven now. You know that."

"But I just heard her. She was that ghost that got in the car with us!"

Her mother shakes her head. "No, baby. That was just part of the ride."

Sloane twists out of her mom's grasp. "No, I heard her!" She bursts into tears and starts running blindly through the park. Her mother runs after her but loses her in the line of people waiting to get on the Peter Pan ride.

*   *   *

Through the walkie-talkie on Mr. Taylor's belt, he is alerted that there's a situation in his vicinity. Still a trainee, his job is to wander between Fantasyland and Liberty Square, keeping his eyes open for trouble. Eventually he'll be stationed at City Hall in the main Guest Relations office. Apparently a crying girl has been sighted running through Liberty Square toward Fantasyland. The girl runs past Mr. Taylor and through Cinderella Castle. He runs after her and radios in his coordinates. When the two of them reach the top of Main Street, she pulls ahead, and his blood freezes. Standing in front of him are Josie and her friends.

"So, Mr. Taylor," Josie's friend Megan says as they all wait for Josie to return from the bathroom. "You, um, work here now?"

He nods. Leave it to Megan to be bold enough to ask. "I just started," he explains. The three of them wait expectantly for him to say more. He sighs and explains that he never loved his job as an accountant, that Josie's turning sixteen made him remember his childhood dream. Saying these words is good practice for when he will repeat them to his family. "Do you girls know what you want to be when you grow up?"

"An actress," Megan says right away, then adds, "An actress who sings. No, a singer who acts!"

"I want to run my own company," Katy says.

"I have absolutely no idea," Zoey answers.

He nods knowingly. "Just remember that life is short, but wide."

"What does that mean?" Zoey asks, but Mr. Taylor doesn't hear her. He's walking briskly toward the little girl who is now emerging from the bathroom.

"I think it means there's more time than you think to explore different things," Katy says.

"Like wearing a polyester vest?" Zoey whispers to Megan.

When the little girl runs out and reaches for Mr. Taylor's hand, he feels a wave of gratitude toward Josie. He knew she'd find the right thing to say. He knew it, even if she didn't.

*   *   *

Tyson and Tom Davis know they should be doing something with their time other than playing video games, but their two older brothers aren't home, and they have to take advantage of the easy access. Their mother wishes they would put more effort into studying, but she has accepted that her twins will never be brain surgeons. They have other gifts, like their gentle, good natures and the way they get joy out of life's simpler pleasures.

When the doorbell rings they call their mom, but she's on the phone and tells them to answer it. Tom reluctantly puts down his joystick and picks up the half-eaten ice pop he had set aside. He opens the door without looking outside first, which he knows he's not supposed to do, but he wants to get back to the game. He is surprised to see Josie Taylor, a girl from school, standing on his front step like it's the most natural thing in the world for her to be doing. She starts talking, but Tom can't seem to focus on her words. He sees Zoey and Megan by the minivan. They scare him a little. They're always telling secrets and giggling.

Tyson wonders what is keeping Tom and bets it's a Girl Scout selling cookies. Last year Tom completely forgot to order the Thin Mints, and there is no way Tyson's going to let that happen again. He hurries to the door. To his surprise, there is no Girl Scout. He eagerly agrees to Josie's proposal. Hanging out with four girls for the afternoon beats playing video games with his brother hands down. Plus it's a nice, warm day and it will be good to be outside.

"Where are we headed?" Tyson asks as we pull away from their house.

"To Celebration," Zoey replies. Then she leans forward and tells Katy and me, "The deli on Celebration Avenue has free papers by the door. I'll run in when we get there. Fifty minutes left!"

I drive a bit too fast into Celebration, which luckily is only two exits off the 417 from the boys' house. As soon as I pass the sign welcoming us to Celebration, I feel like I've left Orlando and entered small-town America. The Disney Company built it to feel that way. The houses are done in a Victorian-meets-the-Old-South style with big wraparound porches and white picket fences. The whole town is really clean and uncluttered. I feel instantly calmer whenever I come here. I pull up in front of the deli so I don't have to find a parking space, and Zoey jumps out. A minute later she's back, empty-handed.

I lean out my window. "What happened?"

"They're all out," she says dejectedly. "The guy said a group of girls came in and took the whole pile."

"Oh, that's just not playing fair," Megan says, hopping out of the car. "C'mon, we'll check the other stores."

Celebration only has four other places to check, so it doesn't take the two of them very long. "All we could find was this." Zoey hands Katy a flyer advertising a town picnic.

"I don't think that's going to cut it."

"Wait a second," I say, turning around to face everyone. "Remember we went to Mr. Simon's house on our Last-Hurrah Halloween? He lives here in town. He must get the paper, right?" I'm already pulling away from the curb as Megan says, "Maybe next Halloween should be the Last Hurrah instead. As I recall, Mr. Simon gave out full-size Snickers."

"Face it, Megan," Zoey says with a sigh. "We're just too old. Last year was embarrassing enough."

A few more turns and we are in front of his house. I turn off the car. "There's no way I'm going in there alone this time."

Katy quickly undoes her seatbelt. "We'll all go."

Everyone piles out of the minivan, including the boys.

"Uh, sorry," Katy says, holding up her hand. "You guys have to wait in the car."

"Can we sit on the curb?" Tyson asks.

"I don't see why not," Katy says. They plop down on the clean white curb and somehow manage to give the impression that they are comfortable. Tyson gently rests Fang's tin on his lap. For teenage boys, they are very well behaved.

We hurry up to the front door and this time Megan rings the bell.

He opens the door and it takes a second for him to recognize us as his students. "To what do I owe this pleasure?" he asks, smiling. "Did you run out of gas?"

"Not exactly," I say. "We sort of need to ask you a favor." He is wearing shorts and a t-shirt and looks even hotter than he does at school.

He steps aside for us to come in. Before he closes the door he says, "Are those the Davis twins?"

I nod.

"Are they coming in too?" he asks.

I shake my head.

He gives them one last look and then closes the door the rest of the way. "So what can I do for you?"

Megan steps forward and blurts out, "We need a copy of the Celebration paper, but we can't tell you why or else that would mean you were helping us and that's against the rules and one of us" — she glances hard at Katy — "is very particular about the rules."

"I think I have it somewhere," he says. "And don't worry, I won't ask any questions." He winks and heads off into another room.

"He's so cute," Megan whispers. "Maybe I'll take photography next year! Should I ask him if he has any Snickers left?"

We all strongly shake our heads.

"Oh my god!" Zoey says loudly, then swiftly lowers her voice. "We could get another item on the list right here!"

"Which one?" Katy asks, confused.

"The underwear from a teacher!"

Megan squeals. "We'd definitely win, then!"

I grab Zoey's arm. "No, we can't do that! What if he catches us? He'll fail me!"

"Don't be such a worrier," Megan says. "I'll run upstairs. It'll only take a second. You can tell him I went to find a bathroom."

Before I can say anything she turns and runs up the stairs.

I lean my head against Katy's shoulder and squeeze my eyes shut. In my head I make a silent plea for Mr. Simon not to come back before Megan returns.

A few seconds later Katy twitches her shoulder and I open my eyes. He's back with the newspaper in his hand. He hands me the paper and looks around. "Where's your other friend?"

My mouth appears unable to function, so Katy gives the excuse. We stand around for another few seconds and then hear a toilet flush upstairs. Good thinking, Megan. She comes down the stairs, her eyes shining. There's a new bulge in the front pocket of her shorts.

"Any problem finding it?" he asks.

Megan grins. "Nope. Second door on the right."

I force myself to speak. "Thanks, Mr. Simon, we've really gotta go."

"See you in class tomorrow, Ms. Taylor," he says as we file past him out the door. "Hi, boys," he calls out to the twins.

"Hi, Mr. Simon," they say together, and stand up when they see us coming.

I clutch the paper so tightly I feel like my hand is going to bleed. We jump in the car and I fumble with the keys. Finally we pull away and around the corner. I put the car in park and turn around to Megan.

"So what did you get? Boxers? Tighty-whities?"

She shakes her head and pulls something black and yellow out of her pocket. "Tada! A leopard-print thong!"

"No way!" Zoey says, grabbing it from her. "This must be Ms. Robinson's, I mean Mrs. Simon's!"

Katy and I just gape. The boys whistle. I guess she isn't as frigid as we all thought!

"Yup. It was either this or the French maid outfit! I figured she'd miss this one less."

"Oh, we are *so* going to win!" Zoey says, bouncing in her seat. "I can't believe she wears that stuff. I'll never look at her in class the same way again!"

"Time check," Katy says.

Zoey checks her watch. "Uh-oh, only twenty minutes left and we still need so many things."

I throw the car into drive and head out of town. Katy takes out her list and crosses off the newspaper and the underwear. "What about the model of a spaceship?"

"Uh, we have one of those," a male voice pops up from the back row.

Katy shakes her head. "Against the rules."

Rob used to have a plastic Star Trek Enterprise hanging from his ceiling in his pre-cool days, but my mother sold it for a dollar at a garage sale last summer. But come to think of it, I saw a spaceship in my house just this morning. "Hey, do you think a piñata shaped like a spaceship counts?"

"I don't see why not," Katy says.

"Do we have time to swing by my house?"

"Just barely," Zoey replies. "Don't you think we have enough stuff to win?"

"We can't be sure," Megan says. "I mean, if someone stole all the newspapers in Celebration, they're playing to win too."

I go as fast as I can without speeding. As we approach my house, Katy points to a Jeep parked in front. "Who's that?"

I pull up next to it, trying to get close enough to see in without scraping the side. Of all people, Grant Brawner is sitting in the passenger seat. His friend Stu is next to him. I pull past them into the empty driveway. No one else is home yet.

"What are they doing here?" Megan asks.

Katy turns to me with wide eyes. "Maybe Grant is going to ask you to the prom!"

"Really? Do you think so?" I glance in the rearview mirror to check how I look. A bit ragged. More than a bit, actually.

"Doubtful," Zoey says.

"Hey, it's possible!" I say indignantly.

"No offense, Josie," she says, "but it's more likely he's here staking out your brother. Waiting for him to show up so they can ambush him with darts. I've seen it before."

"We'll just find out for ourselves," Katy says, getting out of the car. She marches right over there, totally not heeding my begging her not to. I have no choice but to catch up with her. The boys get out of their car when they see us coming. We're like two rival gangs heading toward each other. The two of them, and the six of us, because I forgot for a minute the Davis twins were with us.

"Hey," Grant says to me when we meet on the front lawn.

"Hey," I reply.

"You live here, right?"

"Uh, huh."

"Would it be okay if we used your bathroom?"

Okay, so it wasn't an invite to the prom. "Both of you?"

Stu steps forward. "We drank a lot of Coke running around town this afternoon." He holds up his dart gun. "Gotta have the caffeine to stay on our toes, you know."

Zoey puts her hands on her hips. "Are you going to leave your guns in the car?"

"Sure," Grant says, holding up both hands to show they're empty. "No problem."

"It's okay," I tell them. "Rob isn't home anyway."

Grant looks surprised. "Oh, Rob Taylor is your brother? I hadn't put that together."

Zoey looks doubtful, but I ignore her. Megan is busy checking out Stu.

"You can come in," I tell them. "But we only have two minutes, so you better be fast."

"That's fine," Grant says.

"We really appreciate it," Stu echoes. "It was your house or the woods."

I open the front door and hear that Mom left the television on in the den. She does that sometimes to ward off burglars, since our alarm broke last month. I point out the guest bathroom, and Stu takes off around the corner.

"Wow," Tyson Davis says, taking in all the streamers and signs. "Your parents really do it up for your birthday."

Grant turns to me. "It's your birthday today? Happy birthday."

I can't help but feel a little weak in the knees. "Thanks."

"Fourteen minutes, Josie!" Zoey warns.

I run into the kitchen to get the scissors and hand them to Katy. She reaches up and is about to cut down the piñata when we hear Stu yell, "Gotcha! You're out!"

Rob comes running into the hallway from the den, rubbing his right arm. Stu gives Grant a high five and then takes off again, this time presumably to use the bathroom for real.

"What the hell, Josie?" Rob says angrily. "Why did you let them in the house?"

My mouth falls open. Zoey mumbles, "Told you so."

"But . . . but . . . your car . . . it's not here, and Mom said you were gone." I stumble over my words. "I'm really sorry. If I had known you were home I would never have let them in."

He grabs a juice box from the fridge and slams the door shut. He must really have wanted to win. I haven't seen him this angry in a long time. The Davis twins edge closer to the wall.

"I left the car at Danny's," he says through gritted teeth. "As a decoy."

Just then we hear, in a British accent, "Sod off!" and Danny comes running into the hall, naked except for a pair of graying tighty-whities. Stu follows, his dart gun useless at his side. "Ha!" Danny says triumphantly. "I have foiled your dastardly plot."

Megan starts laughing this big gulping laugh and I cover my eyes. If anyone would take advantage of the underwear clause it would have to be Danny. He doesn't seem to care that we're in the room. The four boys start yelling at each other.

"Seven minutes!" Zoey yells over the din.

Katy hurries and snips the rope, careful not to let the piñata fall. I figure this isn't the best time to ask Rob for a picture of him and Anne kissing. We'll just have to do without that item.

"Put on some clothes, man," Stu says as Danny pushes him and Grant out the door.

"I'm really sorry, Rob," I repeat. I grab the piñata and we run out also.

"It's been that kind of day," he says sadly, shutting the door behind us.

By the time we arrive at Jenny Waxner's house — with two minutes to spare — it's nearly dark out. Her father points us wordlessly to the backyard. Megan holds the duffle, Katy has the piñata securely under her arm, and the boys trail behind with Zoey and me. There must be eighty kids sprawled around the yard, which is lit by big floodlights. We find the poster with our names on it and practically fall to the ground we're so exhausted. The first person I see is Missy Hiver, who looks at the Davis twins and sneers. She actually sneers. Clearly she's jealous that we thought of them first.

Everyone else has their stuff laid out in front of them, so we do the same. I'm amazed at how many things on the list we actually managed to find. I wish it wasn't so crowded so I could see what the other teams got. I'm sure ours is the only spaceship piñata.

Jenny walks through the yard holding a clipboard and conferring with her fellow class officials. When she gets over to us, the first things she sees are the Davis twins. I can tell she's about to ask why they're with our group, when it dawns on her.

"Very good," she says, nodding. "Extra points for creativity."

Zoey nudges Megan and whispers, "Make sure she sees the panties!"

Megan displays them proudly in her outstretched hands. Jenny leans in for a closer look and asks, "Whose are they?"

"Mrs. Simon's!" Megan announces with a flourish.

"Who?"

"You know, Ms. Robinson, the biology teacher?"

"No way!" Jenny says, laughing. Her friends take a closer look too. "How'd you get them?"

"Ah, now that's a secret I'll take to the grave," Megan says. "So, do we win?"

"You'll find out soon enough." She takes inventory of the rest of our stuff and moves on to the next team.

"Look," Katy says, pointing a few teams down. "Amelia is here. I bet her team broke every rule."

We all turn to see Amelia twirling a bra around her finger. She's sitting right under one of the lights, so I can tell it's red. And lacy.

"Whose do you think that is?" I ask.

"It's probably hers," Zoey says. "I'll go find out."

"Ask her if she has any ice cream left," Megan calls out as Zoey weaves her way through the crowd. We watch as Amelia stops twirling when Zoey approaches. The Davis twins have moved a little closer and are watching too. A minute later Zoey returns, clearly disappointed.

"It's real," she says, plopping down. "They got it from the clothesline behind Ms. Connors's apartment."

"People still have clotheslines?" Megan asks.

Katy looks stunned. She must've really hoped Amelia would get caught in a lie. "But if it was a clothesline," Katy reasons, "then how did they know for sure it was hers?"

"They watched her hang it up," Zoey says.

"It's definitely Ms. Connors's," Tom says quietly.

We all turn to stare at him, including his brother.

Tom reddens. "It's no big deal. I was standing at her desk once and she was wearing a really low cut dress and I saw it. Well, the top of it anyway."

Tyson looks impressed. Katy just looks pissed.

"If it makes you feel any better, Katy," Zoey says, "I think they spent so much time getting the bra they didn't get many other things."

"Shh," Megan says. "They're announcing the winners!"

Jenny holds up a battery-operated microphone and says, "You guys did an amazing job. Almost all of you found a copy of the *Kama Sutra,* and may I remind you now to put them back in your parents' nightstands!"

Everyone laughs. She continues. "And many of you realized there are no paper menus at Donald's Hot Dog Hut and found interesting ways to compensate for it, including writing the menu on your stomachs." The guys next to us stand up and pull up their shirts. Megan whistles. "We've tallied up the points and I will distribute the prizes to the winning teams, so stay seated." The four of us grab each other's hands as she makes her way around the yard distributing Sizzler gift certificates to the seven third place winners. She hands the last one to Missy Hiver, who immediately tosses it to her friend Tara like it burns her.

"We have a tie for second place," Jenny announces. Katy grips my hand tighter. I think we'd all be very happy with second place.

Jenny walks past us and hands an envelope to the team of boys with the menus written on their stomachs. They whoop it up and high-five each other. Somehow I can't picture them choosing the spa treatments.

Jenny waves the second envelope in the air and then heads straight for us. She drops it in the middle of our circle. "Congratulations." We drop hands and hug each other. The Davis twins join our group hug even though they can't come with us to the spa.

"I bet if we had just gotten that half-eaten burrito it would have pushed us over the top," Katy says cheerfully, checking her list. "We forgot about that one."

"That's okay, boy bands are so last-century anyway," says Zoey.

Megan holds the envelope high in the air. "Free massages, here we come!"

"Last but certainly not least," Jenny says, "are our first place winners. They got every item on our list, including what must surely be the last bottle of *Gee Your Hair Smells Terrific* in the state of Florida, and, to top it off, these!" She holds up a pair of plain white boxer shorts. "Principal Harrison's boxers!" The team in question jumps up and down, hugging each other. One of the girls is in my math class and she's pretty nice. I'd love to know how they got the boxers. I glance over at Amelia to see how she's handling her defeat. If she didn't look so sad I would gloat.

I drop the Davis twins home with the reminder that lunch is on me tomorrow. After driving around all day I feel like an old pro. As I pull into Katy's driveway Megan exclaims, "Oh my god, we almost forgot to give Josie her present!" She reaches into her pocket and pulls out a small, unsealed envelope with my name on it. "This is from all three of us."

I turn the envelope over in my hand. I can't imagine what's in it.

For a second I wonder if it could be Katy's note from earlier, but that wouldn't make any sense.

"Go ahead," Megan urges. "Open it."

I reach in and pull out a small piece of paper. "Wally's Hot Air Balloons. See the World in a Different Way." I reread it a few times to make sure I am seeing it correctly. Did my friends just give me something that falls into the category of Things That Fall From the Sky?

As believably as I can muster, I exclaim, "Thank you guys, this is great!"

Katy explains, "We figured this would be something you'd like since you're always looking up at the sky. We can all go up together."

Maybe it would have been smart if I had ever explained exactly *why* I'm always looking up at the sky. The picture of the balloon on the card does look really beautiful, though. "When would we do it?"

"We've got a year from today," Megan says.

A whole year to get used to the idea sounds great to me. By the time we get back to Katy's house her mother is home from work and offers to drive me the few blocks home. I grab my bookbag from upstairs and climb back in the minivan, this time in the passenger seat.

"Be ready at eight-thirty for the lake," Zoey calls out as we pull away.

"So," Katy's mom says. "What are you girls actually doing at the lake? Katy won't tell me."

"I honestly don't know. No one will tell me anything either."

She looks doubtful.

"So, did that kid recover from drinking the water?" I ask.

She nods. "He'll have a stomachache for a while."

"What exactly is in that water?"

"Believe me, honey, you don't want to know."

"Uh-oh," I say as my house comes into view. "We have to go back."

"What did you forget?"

"My spaceship."

She raises her eyebrows at me. "Teenagers these days," she says, swinging the car around. "I don't even know what you're talking about half the time."

Missy Hiver and her teammates, Tara, Rachel, and Shira, run into the Celebration Deli and almost knock the newspaper stand over in their hurry to grab a paper.

"I've got an idea!" Missy says. The other girls glance at each other uneasily. Missy's ideas could be dangerous. Shira and Rachel didn't really want to be on her team in the first place. Tara had to convince them that besides an unhealthy obsession with the Olsen twins and a small anger management problem, Missy is really not that bad. Tara doesn't mind being friends with her because she thinks Missy is very lonely.

"Let's take all of them!" Missy says, her eyes gleaming. "That way no one else can get one."

"But that includes anyone who's not in the scavenger hunt," Rachel argues. "The regular people in town couldn't get a paper."

Missy considers this. "What if we promise to return them tonight?"

"It's okay with me," Tara says. Shira and Rachel agree as well, as long as Missy promises to return them. They pile the stacks onto each other's arms and hurry out of the store. Missy opens the trunk of her car, and they drop the newspapers next to Rachel's sister's rejection letter from Florida State (which counts as college letterhead) and a half-eaten burrito that Missy found by fishing through a dumpster behind Taco Haven. It makes the whole car smell, even though it's in the trunk.

The girls pile into the car, and Missy drives a few stores past the deli before she stops. "Let's wait here a few minutes," she suggests. "Just to see another team go in for the papers."

"Five minutes," Tara says. "That's it."

Not even a minute later a blue minivan pulls up in front of the deli and a red-haired girl runs into the store. Missy recognizes Zoey right away. And that means Josie Taylor is behind the wheel of that minivan.

She inches the car forward for a closer look. Sure enough, it's Josie. Now she *knows* she did the right thing by taking all those papers.

Zoey runs back out empty-handed, and even Shira and Rachel have to laugh.

"Let's go now, Missy," Tara says, trying to hide her smile.

Missy slowly approaches the minivan as Megan gets out to join Zoey in a fruitless search. As she drives past, Missy looks in the window of the van and sees, of all things, the Davis twins. She almost doesn't brake in time for the red light ahead of her because she is too busy seething.

"Did you see that?" Missy says, looking behind her at the van. "Those were the Davis twins! I bet they're the two identical things from the list!"

"Gee," Shira says. "Ya think? Too bad you couldn't get Mary-Kate and Ashley, right? Imagine all the bonus points we'd get for them!"

Missy whirls around to face her. Her face is red. "Mary-Kate and Ashley are not identical. Ashley is like, an inch taller!"

Mr. Simon carefully lays the barbell down on the carpet in the spare room he hopes to one day make into a nursery for a baby. He stretches his shoulders and rolls his head from side to side. Before he got married he used to work out much more often. Now he only gets to do it when his wife isn't home or if she's upstairs grading exams. He doesn't really mind, because he doesn't put too much stock in physical appearances. He knows some of the girls at school have crushes on him, and he thinks it's sweet. But rather than worrying about looking buff, he'd rather run through the streets of town or on one of the jogging paths. He loves the feel of the earth beneath his feet, the endorphins kicking in just when he needs them most. He appreciates the peacefulness of his town, but could do without everyone knowing each other's business. Over the weekend he went into Celebration Drugs for constipation medicine, and today three people on the street have asked if his "little problem" was taken care of. Happily, as of second period, all's clear in that area. He felt bad being gone from class for so long, but the laxative wasn't going to wait any longer.

He bends down to pick up the barbell for a second round of reps when the doorbell rings. His wife must have lost her keys again. If he didn't know better, he'd swear she was giving them away to people on the street. He considers taking off his tank top before he answers the door because she told him last week she thought it would be sexy if he greeted her after school with no clothes on. When he opens the door and sees his student and her friends on the stoop, he is immensely glad he decided to remain clothed. Since they are sophomores, he knows they can't be trying to hide from Dart Wars. When one of the girls asks him for a newspaper he remembers that the Sophomore Scavenger Hunt is always on the same day. When he comes back from digging the paper out of the recycling bin, he notices one girl is missing. When she comes downstairs with a noticeable bulge in her pocket, he feigns ignorance and wishes he had remembered to check the Web site to see what she could have taken. When the girls leave he goes straight to the Web site, reads the bonus-points section in horror, and races upstairs to his bedroom. Whew, the French maid outfit is still there. It must not have fit in her pocket. He hopes whatever she took was clean at least.

"How long are we gonna sit here?" Grant Brawner asks Stu. They are parked in Stu's Jeep in front of Rob Taylor's house. Their dart guns lay in their laps, easily accessible if needed.

"Until we figure out a way to get in there," Stu says.

"Can't we just jimmy the lock or something?"

"You know the rules. You can only shoot someone in their house if the door is unlocked or someone lets us in."

"Well, the mother just left, so I say we try again later."

Stu shakes his head. "This is the guy who stole your girlfriend, re-member?"

"Anne was my girlfriend in fifth grade. For two days!" Grant argues. "And we don't even know for sure he's in there."

"Trust me, he's in there. I can smell it."

"I can smell a lot of things in this car, too, and none of 'em are too pretty."

Stu watches in the side mirror as a blue minivan pulls past him. "Speaking of pretty, guess who's home? Little sister."

Grant watches as Josie pulls into the driveway and her friends empty out of a minivan. "There's no way we'll get in now, with all those people."

"You got it wrong, bro. We're totally in now. Just tell your new girl-friend we need to use her bathroom. She'll totally buy it."

"I'm gonna look like a schmuck when she figures it out."

"Dude, it won't be the first time."

Rob and Danny are sprawled on the couches in Rob's den, watching an old *Speed Racer* cartoon on Nickelodeon. Danny now has a new reason to add to the list of why he doesn't want a girlfriend. It sucks when they break up with you. "When did it happen?" he asks Rob.

"After lunch."

"Did you have any clue it was coming?"

"Nope."

"Do you, you know, want to talk about it?"

"Nope."

Danny is relieved. He probably wouldn't be much help. He kicks a couch pillow off to make more room for his legs and as it falls, he hears a noise somewhere in the house. He sits straight up. "Did you hear that?"

Rob shakes his head. "You're paranoid."

"I don't think so," Danny says as the front door opens and a bunch of voices fill the front hall. A second later they hear Josie directing some-one to the bathroom. They gape at each other in a panic. Danny runs into the bathroom in the hall and locks the door. Rob swings himself over the top of the couch in an attempt to hide behind it.

Unfortunately, he's not fast enough, and that jerk Stu nails him in the butt. He knows he shouldn't be so mad at Josie, but he can't help it. He was counting on winning Dart Wars and gaining some of his self-respect back after being dumped. At least Danny's still safe to fight another day. He can always ride his coattails.

Zoey volunteers to go to Amelia's group to ask about the bra. She doesn't really care one iota whose bra it is, but she wants to see if Sara is okay. She feels very protective of her now. Amelia stops twirling long enough to tell Zoey the bra belongs to Ms. Connors. She only half-listens to Amelia's story of how they got it. She's busy trying to catch Sara's eye, but Sara is busy peeling a blade of grass with her fingers. Their other two team members sit as far away from Amelia and Sara as possible while still being on the same team. Zoey leaves, feeling sad for Sara and even a little sad for Amelia. And very grateful for her own friends.

Surrounded by the crowd in Jenny Waxner's backyard, Katy is struck by how comfortable everyone else seems. She's never liked crowds. It makes her feel lonely to be one of so many. She much prefers just being with Josie and Megan and Zoey, or even just Josie. She doesn't mind places like Disney World, where everyone is so spread out (except for weekends and holidays, when she avoids it like the plague). Katy doesn't remember the time she was three years old and her parents took her to a James Taylor concert. Sometime during "Up on the Roof," she wandered off and couldn't see above the knees of the fortysomething baby boomers who had rushed the stage. It wasn't until halfway through "Fire and Rain" that a security guard returned Katy to her parents at the lost-and-found booth. On some level deeper than memory, she is still affected by this experience.

Katy thinks Amelia and her friends crossed the line of fair play when they spied on Ms. Connors. Katy bets that if they had asked, Ms. Connors would have let them borrow the bra. She is glad that Amelia's team didn't even win a free dinner at Sizzler. When the judging is over, everyone is so busy gathering their scavenger hunt items and talking to each other that Katy wanders off unnoticed. She keeps the red bra in her line of sight at all times. As she passes by Amelia's area, she bends down to scratch her knee and scoops the bra into her fist, glad for the first time that her hands are so large. Pivoting on her heel, she makes her way back to her own team. She will make sure that Ms. Connors gets her property back, a promise she bets Amelia wouldn't keep.

Jeff Grand stops walking in front of Jenny Waxner's house and sees all the cars parked out front. Some of them have parents or older siblings waiting at the wheel. He knows a lot of kids in his grade are at Jenny's right now. If his parents could have adjusted their shifts at the Animal Kingdom, maybe he'd be there too. Chances are he'll need to ask Josie for her homework again, since he'll be watching his sister for the rest of the day. Right now he is pulling her behind him in a red wagon that she has almost outgrown.

"Is a pahty?" Sage asks, looking up at him with her wide blue eyes.

"Yes," Jeff tells her, kneeling at the side of the wagon. "It's a party."

She reaches out her hand and grabs his chin. "Home now?"

Jeff stands up and grabs the wagon handle. Without another glance at Jenny's house, he says, "Yeah. Home now."

When Tom and Tyson return home, Tyson heads for the fridge and Tom goes up to the room that the two of them share. Next year, when their next-older brother goes away to school, they'll each get their own room. Tom knows that's supposed to be a good thing, but he worries he'll be lonely. He takes out the small sketchbook that he uses as a diary and begins writing his daily entry. He is very proud of his penmanship.

February 29th. Leap Day. Except for my negatives being blank
in photography class this morning, it's been a really good day.

I didn't throw up.

I didn't get a splinter.

I didn't say anything stupid.

I didn't poke myself in the eye with the end of my pen.

I didn't fail the surprise math quiz.

I didn't trip on my shoelaces in gym.

I didn't have pizza stuck in my teeth after lunch.

I didn't blush when girls spoke to me, except for a few times but that really couldn't be helped because of all the girls around me this afternoon at the scavenger hunt which really isn't the usual scenario.

It doesn't occur to Tom to write the things that he *did* do today. He won't start writing those things in his diary until next year, when he'll start calling it a journal. He'll have had his own room for months by then, along with a new appreciation of why a teenage boy might *want* his own room.

Katy decides not to go along for the ride while her mother takes Josie home. She wants to take a bath and think for a while before she has to go out again to the lake. She smiles to herself as she climbs out of her shorts. Out of twenty teams, she and her friends tied for second place. That's a pretty amazing achievement. Katy loves that the four of them don't compete with each other for the leadership role. They all compliment each other. This willingness of Katy's to step up to the plate, to see the greater picture and to break it down accordingly, will serve Katy well for the rest of her life. She helps others to be their best, without anyone consciously realizing it.

Katy climbs into the tub and lets the water cover everything except her face and ears. Luckily the tub is extra-long, so she can almost completely straighten her legs. She loves the peacefulness of the bath and the thick weight of the water on her skin. She goes over the day in her mind. That whole thing with the note and Mrs. Lombardo was surreal. Seeing

Josie's dad, the mild-mannered accountant, working at Disney World was even more surreal. Katy wonders if Josie realizes how lucky she is that her father actually asked for her help. Her own father is a surgeon at Orlando General, and she rarely sees him. She can't remember the last time the two of them did anything together. His birthday is coming up in a few weeks. Maybe she'll surprise him and write him a poem. She lets her whole head sink under the water for a second until she hears the roaring in her ears. *Nah. I'll just get him a tie, as usual.*

The first thing I see when I walk up to my front door is a big poster with CONGRATULATIONS, NEW DRIVER! written in red marker. Underneath is a drawing of the Shark that looks like it was done by a five-year-old. If Dad's latest career doesn't work out, at least he can cross "professional artist" off the list. When I get inside I'm greeted with the sight of Grandma holding the end of a piece of yellow yarn. The rest is pulled taut around the corner.

"Whatcha doing, Grandma?" I ask, giving her a kiss on the cheek. I lay the piñata and my books against the stairs.

"Hi, baby," she says. "Rob asked me to hold this end of yarn while he measures something down the hall."

I try not to laugh. "How long have you been standing here?"

"Oh, I don't know, maybe ten minutes?"

Now I can't help it. "Ten minutes? Grandma, it's a practical joke. Rob tied the other end to a table or something. He's waiting to see how long you'll stand there. C'mon, I'll show you."

Reluctantly she follows me around the corner and into the den, where, just as I said, the yarn is tied to the leg of the coffee table.

"Come out, you scoundrel!" Grandma orders. Rob and Grandpa come out from behind the couch. Rob is holding his stomach from laughing so hard. Grandpa has his usual glass of whiskey in his hand and a satisfied smile on his face. Rob is certainly in a better mood than the last time I saw him.

"I should have known you'd be involved in this, Harold," Grandma says, shaking her head. "Oh, the jokes he used to pull on my parents when we were young."

My grandfather is a walking contradiction. He used to be an

accountant, like my father, and it took a small heart attack at seventy to get him to retire. He drinks a shot of whiskey a day, and doesn't suffer fools gladly, as he'll tell anyone who will listen. Yet he's been pulling quarters out of our ears and encouraging us to fill the sugar bowl with salt for as long as I can remember.

He gives me a hug, and I can feel how thin he has gotten. As much as I love them, seeing my grandparents always reminds me of how much I don't want to get old.

Mom walks into the den, carrying the piñata. "I wondered where this had gone. How'd you guys do?"

"Second place," I tell her and follow her back out to the hall. She stands on the step stool and hangs the piñata back up. It sways back and forth and almost bonks her on the head.

"That's great," she says, ducking. "Hey, how did the muffins go over?"

I don't have the heart to tell her that someone stole them. "Great. All that was left were crumbs."

"Good." She folds up the stool and goes back to making dinner.

I grab my bag and run up to my room. I desperately want to squeeze in a shower before the pizza comes. I need to talk to Dad, too. The doorbell rings just as I hide the purple tube of Breast Boost in the nightstand. No shower for the sweaty and stinky, apparently.

"Josie," Dad calls up. "Come on down." I quickly throw off my white t-shirt and put on the new red one with THE FEW, THE PROUD, THE LEAPERS on it. It seems appropriate. I head downstairs, where everyone is gathered by the door. The pizza boxes are sitting on the landing of the stairs, so I carefully step over them.

"Hurry, Josie," my mother says when she sees me. "We've been waiting for you." The Domino's guy has a paper scroll open in his hands. I had forgotten about this part. He clears his throat.

"May this very special day bring you four more years of good tidings, good health, good friends, and good pizza. Happy Leap Day Birthday from Domino's."

He rolls up the scroll, hands it to me, and says, "See you in four years."

Dinner goes like this: Free pizza on the good china. Side dish of french fries and a bowl of vanilla ice cream for dipping, which Mom usually dissuades me from doing, but on my birthday allows. Grandma asks Grandpa if he really needs that second glass of whiskey. Grandpa asks Dad how his mutual funds are doing. Dad says fine and throws me pleading glances that I read as *Please don't say anything about today.* Mom asks me if I feel older, and I say that I'm beginning to. Rob is quiet and doesn't speak to anyone except to ask for more pizza. Dad asks Grandma if she's remembering to take gingko biloba for her memory. Mom asks Rob if any of his friends have heard back from the colleges they applied to. He grunts and shrugs.

Mom and I clear the plates and pile them on the counter by the sink. "So," she says, pulling on her yellow gloves. "I hear you had quite the adventure this afternoon."

"The scavenger hunt? Yeah, it was pretty crazy."

"No, I mean with your dad."

I nearly drop the plate I'm holding. "When did he tell you?"

"Just before you came home."

"Do Grandma and Grandpa know?"

She shakes her head and leans in close. "And don't tell them. He'll do it when he's ready."

Dad ducks his head in the kitchen. "Who's ready for presents?"

Hey, I don't need to be called twice when presents are being offered. I pull him aside on our way into the den.

"Are we going to talk about this?" I whisper.

"Tomorrow, okay, honey? It's been a long day."

I'm slightly disappointed that he doesn't want to confide in me. "Okay."

"I'm very proud of how well you helped today. If you want a job in my department over the summer, I'm sure you'd get it."

"Hopefully I'll be Snow White, remember?"

"Yes, of course. Well, c'mon, these presents aren't going to open themselves."

I sit on the den couch like a queen on the throne, and one by one people hand me presents. I should turn sixteen more often. This is what I get: Rob gives me an assortment of car stuff, including a mini Dustbuster, a portable cup holder (the Shark is so old there isn't one built in), a battery-operated radio (the Shark only gets AM), and a pair of sunglasses so that, as he put it, I can at least try to pass for cool. My parents give me sixteen-dollar gift certificates to The Gap, Express, Old Navy, Taco Bell, and Mobil Gas. I know money is tight, and I hadn't expected anything from them after the key to the car this morning. Grandma surprises me with a pink-and-white box from Victoria's Secret. Inside is a pair of beautiful red silk pajamas that slide through my fingers like butter. According to the card, every sixteen-year-old should have a pair of silk pajamas. How cool is Grandma?

Mom agrees to let me take a quick shower before dessert, so I scoop up all my new goodies and deposit them on the bed on top of all my school stuff. I can't wait to wear the pajamas tonight. So that I don't forget later, I take a minute to send off an email to Niki. It must be my lucky day because her name comes up on my IM buddy list.

Josie229: Happy Leap Day Birthday! My boobs thank you for the gift!

Nikster: Uh, sorry. This is Niki's dad. Let me go get her.

I stare at the screen. NOOOO!! I want to crawl under my desk.

Nikster: just kidding, Josie. it's me.

Josie229: oh, you are in so much trouble!

Nikster: glad you liked the gift. you'll have to let me know if it works.

Josie229: i will. my friends are taking me to one of the lakes in Orlando for this surprise birthday initiation thing. I'm a little scared.

Nikster: hey, i have to go, the pizza just got here and my mom is yelling for me to come downstairs so the guy can do the whole scroll thing. i'm sure you'll have a great time at the lake. remember, these are your friends, they're not going to make you do anything you don't want to. leapest regards, Niki.

Her name disappears from my buddy list before I can respond. I'm about to head to the bathroom when Grandma appears at my door.

"I have one more gift for you," she says, placing a small green velvet box in my hand.

My mom once told me the smaller the box, the better the present. She's definitely right this time, because inside the box is the most beautiful ring I've ever seen. The band is gold and the rectangular stone is purple. When I tilt it, the light refracts in the stone.

"Is this really mine?" I ask, searching her face.

She nods. "The stone is an amethyst. Try it on."

I lift the delicate ring out of the box and slip it on. It's a little big, but if I don't shake my hand too much it stays on. Grandma sits at the end of the bed and I sit down next to her, unable to take my eyes off the ring.

"When I was sixteen," she says, "my grandmother gave me that ring. Now I'm giving it to you."

"But I've never seen you wear it before." I hold it closer to my face. It looks brand new.

"I only wore it until I got married. Then I put it away for my own granddaughter until her sixteenth birthday. Maybe you'll do the same."

I can't even form a picture in my mind of me with a granddaughter. "What if I never have one?"

"You will," she says, stroking my hair.

"I think I need a boyfriend first, Grandma."

She laughs. "You'll have a few of those too. I better let you take that shower or your mother will scold me for holding up dessert."

She gives me a big hug and I thank her for the ring.

"It brings all good things to the wearer," she says as she leaves me.

I tilt my finger and watch the reflection of my room reveal itself in the surfaces of the ring. This is the nicest gift anyone has ever given me. I check the clock. It's already 8:00! I hurry into the bathroom, throw off my clothes, and jump in the shower. I have to be careful not to get my hair wet since I don't have time to dry it again. Taking two showers in one day is unusual for me. But this whole day has been unusual, so it seems only fitting.

I feel revived after my shower. Back in my room I throw on jeans and my leaper shirt again. My hair gets a quick brushing, lipstick is smeared on, ring glints on my finger, and I'm ready to go.

Rob comes in to get me, sent by Mom. He sits down on the end of the bed, right where Grandma had been. He almost never comes all the way into my room like this. The whole pinkness issue.

"I wanted to apologize for getting so mad this afternoon," he says. "It really wasn't about the stupid Dart Wars."

I walk over and stand in front of him. "What was it about, then?"

He doesn't answer, just pulls at the hair on his legs, a habit that I've never understood. "Anne broke up with me today."

My mouth falls open. "Are you serious? I saw you guys at lunch and everything seemed great."

He shakes his head. "She broke up with me in the parking lot."

"Why? I thought you guys were so happy together."

"We were," he says. "At least I was. She said it was getting too serious. I think Sherri Haugen's whole baby thing freaked her out."

"Do you think you'll get back together?"

He shakes his head. "I don't think so. I called her and she didn't pick up. She hasn't called back."

I reach over and put my hand on his arm. "I'm really sorry."

He just nods. Then he asks, "Where did you get that ring?"

I lift up my hand and let the stone catch the light again. "From Grandma. It used to be hers."

"I thought maybe some guy at school gave it to you."

That stops me in my tracks. "What guy would give me a ring?"

He shrugs. "I don't know."

"We better go down now," I tell him, walking toward the door.

He nods again but doesn't move. I leave him and go downstairs. I think it's going to be a long time until some guy gives me a ring. My eyes open wide when I see the dining room table. The whole thing is covered with cakes and pies and cupcakes. Enough to feed an army. An army with a big sweet tooth. When I get closer I see there are birthday candles stuck in each one, but they're not lit yet. My mom has a big grin on her face.

"Mom, who's gonna eat all this?"

"Your friends will help when they get here. We can freeze the rest."

I try to figure out how I'm ever going to come up with enough wishes when from the kitchen I hear Grandpa boom, "And you're going to support your family on *that*? That's absurd!"

"Oh, hush, Harold," my grandmother says. "Let him do what he wants."

In response to Grandpa's comment Dad says loudly, "It's none of your business how I support my family."

"It sure as heck will be my business when you can't come up with the mortgage because you're off making happy with the tourists!"

Mom and I exchange horrified looks. Dad and Grandpa may not be very close, but I've never heard them yell at each other before.

Just then the doorbell rings. "Saved by the bell," Mom says, and goes to answer it. Katy, Zoey, and Megan pour in, followed, oddly enough, by Zoey's brother, Dennis, who glances around awkwardly. The girls notice my new ring right away and cluster around to admire it. Zoey tilts her head slightly toward her brother and whispers, "He's our ride."

Rob comes downstairs. He sees Dennis and says, "Hey."

"Hey," replies Dennis, before quickly looking away again.

Mom announces we all have to sit around the table for dessert. I can still hear Dad and Grandpa arguing in the kitchen, although they've lowered their voices.

"Uh, we really have to go, Mom," I tell her, pointing at my watch.

"We have a few minutes," Megan says. "You can't miss dessert on your birthday!"

"Thank you, Megan," my mother says, putting her arm around Megan's shoulders.

"Yeah, thanks, Megan," I whisper as we gather around the table. I really don't want to deal with my family fighting while my friends — and Zoey's weird brother who I've never said more than ten words to — are here. Dad and Grandma come out of the kitchen with strained smiles on their faces and greet everyone. Grandpa isn't smiling at all. Mom leans over the table and lights all the candles with one of those long automatic lighters you use to light a grill. She switches off the lights and everyone sings "Happy Birthday."

"Make a wish," my friends clamor. "Make a wish!"

"But there are ten candles!" I seriously cannot come up with ten wishes. "I have an idea," I announce. "Everyone get in front of a candle and at the same time we'll all make wishes."

"Are you sure, honey?" Mom asks, her old guilt at giving birth to me on Leap Day resurfacing.

I nod. "Okay, everyone close your eyes, make a wish, and blow." Eyes shut all around the table except for Grandma and me. Grandma winks at me and then closes hers. It's weird that I'll never know what they are all wishing for. Ms. Connors once told us that ninety-five percent of the time that we think we know what someone is thinking, we are wrong. I close my eyes and wish that I never forget this day, my last Leap Day birthday as a teenager. Who knows, I could be alone for my twentieth in four years. Just me and the Domino's Pizza guy, who no doubt will find me wherever I am. I blow out the candle and watch the other ones go out around me. Everyone claps.

Mom makes us each a plate of assorted desserts, giving Megan the biggest plate of all. Once we've scarfed down the food and my friends have dutifully answered every question put to them by my parents, Mom says, "Oh no, we forgot the piñata!"

"Can't we do it tomorrow?" I ask, edging toward the door. It's embarrassing enough that I have a piñata and I'm not in kindergarten, but to have everyone watch is just too much.

"Come on, Josie," Katy says, picking up the Wiffle bat that is leaning against the wall. "Take a whack at it."

"Yeah, come on," someone else adds.

"Fine, but I'm not being blindfolded." I step under the spaceship and close my eyes. Katy stands behind me and turns me around three times. Totally dizzy, I swing the bat and hit nothing but air. Everyone laughs. I try again and my bat grazes the ship. I open my eyes and put my hand against the banister to steady myself.

"Okay, game over," I say. "We're leaving now."

"I want to try," Megan says, taking the bat from me. I sigh and sit down on the stairs next to Rob. I'm glad my birthday can help him take his mind off Anne. Katy has established herself as the official twirler. Megan does only slightly better than I did. She hands the bat to Zoey, who actually makes a thin crack in the side. Grandma steps up for a turn. Katy only spins her around once, which was very thoughtful. Grandma swings once and hits the same spot Zoey had. Everyone claps as a roll of Smarties and two Starbursts fall to the floor. Grandma hands the bat to Dennis, who looks unsure.

"Go on, young man," she says. "Show us what you've got."

Katy spins Dennis around three times and he doesn't swing right away like everyone else. He adjusts his feet slightly like he's tuning in to the spaceship's location. Then he lifts his bat and whales on the thing. It cracks wide open and the candy falls out all over him and splashes onto the floor. A cheer rises up as we all scramble for the candy like we're five years old.

"Remember," Grandma whispers to me as I hoard my candy into the plastic bag my mother handed out. "You don't stop playing when you get old, you get old when you stop playing."

Why haven't I ever noticed how wise my grandmother is?

Finally, we're ready to leave. I'm very pleased to see that Megan didn't ask to use the bathroom after she ate all the desserts. Hopefully I was wrong about that whole thing. As I'm about to close the front door behind us, Rob yanks me back in.

"If you don't want Dennis to take you home," he says, "call me and I'll pick you up."

I watch as Dennis opens the passenger door for his sister to get in. "I think it'll be okay, but thanks for the option. Last chance to tell me what's going to happen at the lake."

Rob shakes his head. "Just be glad there's no full moon tonight."

"Wait," I call out as he closes the door and locks it. "What does that mean?"

Rob clicks through the channels aimlessly while his grandfather pours himself a glass of whiskey from the cabinet. Usually by this time he'd be starving and waiting outside for the pizza man, but he doesn't have an appetite tonight.

"Anything good on?" his grandfather asks.

"Nah."

"It's a woman, isn't it?"

Rob's finger stops mid-click. "What's a woman?"

"A woman that's got you so blue." He lowers himself slowly onto the couch.

"How'd you know?"

"A kid your age, it's either about girls or sports, and I know football season is over. So, what happened?"

"My girlfriend dumped me."

"She'll be back," he says. "You call her and talk sense into her."

"Maybe later," Rob says.

"I know what will cheer you up. A practical joke. I got an oldie but a goodie in mind."

"That's okay, Grandpa. I'm not really in the mood."

"Trust me."

Five minutes later Rob hands his grandmother the end of a long piece of yarn and asks her to hold it for a minute. Grandpa had told him to tell her something as technical as possible so she won't ask too many questions. He thinks for a minute and tells her he has to measure the square footage of that part of the house to see how far the stereo speakers will project sound. Rob backs away from her, unspooling the rest of the yarn, and pulls it tautly around the corner, down the hallway, and into the den where his grandfather directs him to tie it around the leg of the coffee table. They go to hide behind the couch, Rob supporting his grandfather so his knees won't ache. Every once in a while Rob can't contain a chuckle and it slips out.

"You're right," he whispers. "I do feel better."

"I'm sorry, I think I misunderstood you," Josie's mom whispers to her husband as they set the dining room table for Josie's birthday dinner. "It sounded like you said you got a job at Disney World as a part-time guest relations host for eight dollars an hour, and that Josie helped you this afternoon."

"I did," Jonathan whispers back. They are whispering so Josie's grandmother, who for some reason is standing in the hall holding a piece of yarn, won't hear. Josie's dad carefully places a fork on the center of a napkin and avoids his wife's eyes. "It was a childhood dream of mine." He figures saying that will make it harder for her to argue with him; after all, who doesn't want their loved ones' childhood dreams to come true?

Josie's mom watches her husband, whom she thought she knew everything about by now. "Why didn't you tell me this sooner?"

"It all happened so fast," he explains.

"You're still looking for a real job, though, right?" she asks, holding her breath.

"Yes, of course," he readily assures her. "In fact I have an interview next Thursday."

She isn't sure whether to believe him, so she manages a smile and hurries off to check the stove. Everything around her feels a little unfamiliar.

Andy Moraniz shifts his weight onto one leg and balances the three pizza boxes on his opposite hip. With his free hand he rings the bell at the Taylor residence. He couldn't believe it when they told him at the store that his next delivery included having to give a speech. As the door opens he finds himself wondering if he'll still get a tip, since the pizzas are free. Andy thinks it's a pretty good deal that all you have to do is be born on a certain day and *BAM*, free pizza for life. When he and his fiancée get married, they've already decided to plan it so their baby will be born on Leap Day.

Josie's mom watches her family at dinner and wishes they could see themselves as she sees them. Her husband keeps brushing his hand against the shirt pocket, where his new plastic name tag is hidden; Rob is chewing slowly and his eyes are downcast; and Josie dips her french fries in ice cream like it's the most normal thing in the world. Even with so many people around, Josie is inside her own head, as usual, watching everything but only seeing half of it.

Watching his sister open her gifts gets Rob's mind off of Anne. Josie takes such a childlike joy in the process. First she examines each item while it's still in the wrapping paper. He can practically see the gears turning inside her head as she tries to figure out what the present is. Then she rips off the paper and tosses it in the air in her hurry to get at the present. Mom scoops the wrapping paper up and tries to salvage what's left in case she needs to use it some day. In fact, the gift certificates from Mom and Dad are wrapped in the recycled green-and-red paper from last Christmas. When the pile has been exhausted, everyone leaves the room except Rob and his grandfather.

"Call her," his grandfather demands.

"Now?"

"Now."

He pushes himself up from the floor. "I don't think it will do any good."

"Call who?" his grandmother asks, coming back into the room with a small bag. She must have forgotten to give Josie one of her presents.

"The pope," his grandfather answers.

His grandmother turns to Rob and says, "It should be crystal clear that I didn't marry your grandfather for his sense of humor."

Josie's grandmother leaves the two alone in the den and slowly ascends the stairs. From Josie's doorway, she watches Josie typing away on the computer. She and Josie are so much alike, and so different. Sometimes when she looks at her she sees the ghost of herself at that age. So much ahead of her. So many joys and disappointments. Of course, in her day at sixteen you already knew your future. In the next few years you'd get married, have babies, and maybe be a teacher or a nurse if you had to work outside of the house. But Josie has the whole world at her feet. The odd thing is, she doesn't envy her granddaughter's options. Life today is a lot more complicated.

She watches Josie's face light up when she sees the ring. Giving it away after forty-six years is both a strange and satisfying feeling. Her jeweler did such a wonderful cleaning job that no one would guess it wasn't brand new. Before he put it back in the box she had tried to put it on. It wouldn't fit, although she tried every finger. They were too swollen with age.

Rob wants to be as far away from the rest of the family as possible when he makes the call. He could take his cell phone out to the Shark, but since that was the place she dumped him, it probably wouldn't bring very good karma. He decides to use the phone up in his parents' room. He sits on his mom's side of the bed and stares at the phone. Now or never. He picks it up, dials the number, and immediately hangs up. This wouldn't be a problem if Anne didn't have caller ID. But since of course she does, he now has to call back or look like an idiot.

He paces the room, and as he passes his father's dresser he sees a folder on top marked "Guest Relations." He opens the folder and flips absently through the pages. Anything to avoid making the phone call. It takes him a few seconds to realize what he's looking at. "Magic Kingdom New Hire Training Schedule" with "Jonathan Taylor" written on the top. He always knew his dad was a little strange, but what the heck is all this?

He hears Josie turn on the shower and knows he has to hurry and make the call while she's still in there. He shuts the folder and makes sure it's in the same position on the dresser. He calls Anne's number again, this time letting it ring. After four rings, her machine picks up. Not having prepared for that outcome, he babbles something along the lines of, "Rob, it's Anne, I mean, obviously I mean Anne, it's Rob. I really want to talk about today, or see you, whichever, or talk, that's fine. Okay? Call me." He places the phone back in the cradle and shakes his head. It was nice while it lasted. How many people wind up spending their life with their first girlfriend anyway?

Anne sits on her bed and listens to Rob's voice as he leaves his message. Her hand reaches toward the phone but she jerks it back. Just hearing his voice, deep and pleading and sad, makes her doubt her decision. The blinking red light on the answering machine stares up at her like an accusing eye. Before she can change her mind, Anne leans over and presses the delete button. She then walks purposefully down the hall, past her bathroom, past her parents' bedroom, and into the kitchen. She opens the refrigerator, roots through the bottom shelf, and grabs an onion. The outer layer peels off easily. She turns it around in her hands until the smell stings her eyes and she has to blink a few times to clear them. Then she bites into it hard, like it was an apple.

After dinner, when Josie asks all of them to make a wish, Rob wishes he'll get over Anne soon so he won't be the only football player sitting home on prom night. Josie's grandmother wishes she could stop the aging process, since she still feels sixteen. Josie's grandfather wishes for regular bowel movements. Josie's father wishes that he'll win Disney Employee of the Month. Josie's mom wishes mothering teenagers came with a handbook. Katy wishes Josie will still be her friend after they talk about the note. Zoey wishes that she'll get some action at the lake tonight. Megan wishes she gets to be Belle, and that Josie gets to be Juliet. She also wishes that the guy Zoey is setting her up with at the lake tonight will like her. Dennis wishes that he hadn't sold that bag of oregano to those college guys claiming it was weed. He also wishes that they won't figure it out until they are far away from Orlando.

Rob sits on the steps and watches as Katy takes control of the piñata game. He thinks she is a good influence on his sister. Katy seems to have it all together and is usually the one to take charge in the group. She laughs as she twirls Megan around, and Rob wonders why he never noticed that she has a very throaty, sexy laugh.

As everyone else is scrambling to get the candy into their bags, Rob pulls Dennis aside and tells him to keep an eye on things at the lake. Since no one ever entrusts Dennis with such things, he readily agrees. As much as he hates to admit it, Dennis is jealous of Rob and Josie's relationship. Of their whole family, actually. They truly seem to like each other. Rob and Josie would never set a Port-a-Potty on fire. They wouldn't need to. He decides he's glad that Zoey blackmailed him into driving her friends tonight by threatening to tell their parents he changed every grade on his last report card. He knows she swiped his cigarettes from under the bed. When her friends aren't around, he plans to warn her not to start smoking. It turns out he won't need to.

Before I squish into the back of Dennis's old Pontiac next to Katy and Megan, I look up at the sky. Only a half moon tonight. I wish I knew why that is a good thing. I close the door behind me and quickly roll down the window because the car smells like old cigarettes and fast food hamburgers. The *Playboy* air freshener hanging from the rearview mirror isn't helping. I notice Zoey has a backpack on her lap in the front seat. Even though it doesn't make any sense why she would have brought it, I lean forward and ask, "Is that the scavenger hunt stuff?"

Zoey shakes her head. "Just some supplies for tonight."

I turn to Katy. I am trying to sound casual, but my heart is thumping. "Supplies? For what?"

Katy gets all wide-eyed and innocent. "Don't ask me."

Maybe someone else in this car will tell me something. In my sweetest voice, I ask, "Dennis, can you tell me what's going to happen at the lake?"

"Not even if I wanted to," he says, turning left onto Orange Avenue toward Lake Eola. "No one brought me for my sixteenth birthday."

"Oh." And then, so that he won't feel bad — okay, so *I* won't feel as bad — I say, "You're lucky."

He doesn't respond. We're now passing through the area of town with all the funky clothes shops and music stores and lots of bars and clubs. It's pretty quiet out right now, but on the weekends there are lots of people in the streets, and my mother used to never let me hang out here. Now that I have my license, I can come down here whenever I want. I still can't believe it.

As we approach the lake, Dennis makes a few turns and then pulls off onto a gravel road that I've never noticed before.

I ask why we're going this way.

"We're actually not going to Lake Eola," Zoey says. "We need a place a little more hidden."

"Great," I mutter.

Katy pats my hand. It doesn't help.

A good ten minutes later we turn off the road and into a little parking lot area with a lot of trees. I can't even see the lake from here. Besides us, there are only four other cars.

"I thought it would be more crowded," I say as we get out of the car.

"Well, it is a Monday night," Megan says.

"Dennis," Zoey says, swinging the bag over her shoulder. "You can stay with the car if you want." She is clearly hoping he'll agree.

He shakes his head. I'm actually kind of relieved. It's very dark out.

"Suit yourself," Zoey says. "But you're not sitting with us." She gestures for us to follow her and heads right into the woods.

"No way," I say, stopping at the edge of the parking lot. "There could be snakes in there."

"There are no snakes," Megan says, pushing me forward. "It's only a two-minute walk." Everyone else is already far ahead so I see no choice but to follow. The leaves and branches crunching under my feet make me very glad I'm wearing thick sneakers. I'm also glad I'm wearing jeans and not shorts. God knows what kinds of creepy, crawly things are in here. Everyone else is laughing and having a grand time trampling through the woods in the dark. I wish I could be like that. I don't care what Rob said, I wish there was a full moon. That way it wouldn't be so dark and every tree wouldn't look like something out of a nightmare.

My eyes are just starting to adjust to the dark when we step out into a big clearing. About fifty feet in front of us sits a lake not as big as Eola, but I can still only barely see the other side of it. The surface of the water reflects the trees around it and the stars and moon above.

"See?" Zoey says. "Wasn't it worth the scary walk through the woods?"

I grudgingly agree. It's much lighter here because scattered around the beachfront are small bonfires with groups of two to four people around them.

Zoey points to one with two boys. "There they are," she says, and starts walking toward them, the bag bouncing on her shoulder. Megan hurries after her, and Dennis wanders off to start his own bonfire on the other side of the clearing.

"Who are these people?" I ask Katy as we trudge slowly behind Zoey and Megan.

"Zoey met one of them a few weeks ago. They go to Orlando South."

I walk even slower. Hanging out with strange guys doesn't exactly thrill me. "Katy, in case this is our last moment alone, remember that you promised to give me that note tonight. Or at least tell me what was in it."

"I know. You haven't let me forget for a second."

We reach the bonfire and sit down on the hard-packed sand. Zoey introduces us to Marc and Justin, juniors at Orlando South. I prefer to think of them as Joe and Shmo. They are both blond, very preppy, and judging by the empty beer bottles next to them, not very sober. Megan is sitting very close to Shmo, so I can only assume that Joe is the one Zoey likes.

"They were supposed to bring two friends," Zoey explains as she unzips her backpack.

"It's really okay," Katy insists.

"Yes," I add. "No problem at all." Even though my infatuation with Grant has been severely tested this afternoon, I'm relieved I don't have to deal with being set up with anyone.

The first thing Zoey pulls out of her bag is a huge Hershey's chocolate bar. Maybe the big ritual is making s'mores, and they got me all nervous for nothing. Zoey rests the chocolate on her leg and reaches back into the bag. This time she pulls out a stack of plastic cups and a tall dark bottle. I lean closer and read the label. HIRAM WALKER BLACKBERRY BRANDY. The last time I checked, s'mores were made with chocolate, graham crackers, and marshmallows. No brandy anywhere in the ingredients. Katy and I exchange glances. The only alcohol we've ever had was champagne on New Year's Eve once with Katy's parents. Megan doesn't seem surprised to see the brandy. She must have been in on it.

Zoey passes a cup to each of us and unscrews the top of the brandy bottle. "First we need to toast Josie's fourth birthday."

"Huh?" Joe says. "How can it be her fourth birthday?"

"Because my birthday is today," I explain. "February twenty-ninth."

"I don't get it," Shmo says.

"You know, Leap Day? Only once every four years?"

"Ohhh," Joe says. "Cool."

"That sucks," Shmo says. "You're not gonna be twenty-one for, like, ever."

"It's a burden," I sigh dramatically. "But I've learned to live with it."

Katy punches me and I try not to laugh.

"Okay, enough of that," Zoey admonishes us. "We have to get down to business." She stands up and goes around the circle, filling each of our cups halfway.

I bring the cup to my nose and sniff it. Kind of fruity.

"Wait," Megan says. "Don't forget the chocolate."

"Oh yeah." Zoey hurries to unwrap the big bar. Then she breaks off a little piece and drops one in each of our cups. "This is supposed to make it taste better. To Josie," she says, holding her cup out in front of her. "Happy birthday to one of the best people I know."

Aw, shucks. We all tap our cups together, except for the boys who are already guzzling theirs down. I tentatively bring the cup to my lips and peek over the edge to watch my friends. Megan and Zoey have already taken a sip and have almost identical grimaces on their faces. I turn to Katy.

"Bottoms up," she says and takes a big swig. Then she grabs her throat and says something that sounds like, "*Achachahhhh.*"

Not very inspired by anyone's reactions, I take a very small sip and then a slightly larger one. It burns my throat a little, but feels slightly warm too. It sure tastes bad though. Megan and Zoey are both forcing themselves to take some more sips, but Katy and I have put ours down in the sand. I reach in and pull out the chocolate to suck on. It didn't seem to help the taste of the brandy. And the taste of the brandy sure hasn't helped the taste of the chocolate. I toss it into the fire where it quickly melts into a brown puddle.

"Anyone got any cigarettes?" Joe asks.

To my great surprise, Megan digs into her sweatshirt pocket and pulls out a pack of Marlboro Lights. She hands them to Joe.

"Since when did you start smoking?" I ask her. "Belle does not smoke."

"Why would a bell smoke?" Shmo asks.

I'm about to answer but decide it's not worth it.

Megan says, "Don't worry, I'm not smoking."

"I'll try one," Zoey says. Joe pulls one out and hands it to her.

"Does anyone have any matches?" Joe asks. "Or a lighter?"

"You don't have any?" Katy asks. "How did you start the fire?"

"We used a match. But after we lit the fire we threw the pack in to watch them pop."

Zoey solves the problem by sticking the end of her cigarette directly into the fire. She pulls it out and the entire bottom half is black.

"Hurry and toke on it," Joe instructs her. "Or it won't catch."

She puts the cigarette to her lips and inhales deeply. The end catches just like Joe said it would. But Zoey's face turns bright red. I'm waiting for the smoke to come out of her mouth. Suddenly she starts coughing and hacking and her eyes water. Megan leans over and pounds her on the back. Zoey waves her off, holding her throat.

"Will a sip of this help?" Joe asks, holding out the brandy.

"Uh, I don't think so," Katy says.

Zoey finally stops coughing and buries the cigarette in the sand. "Well, that's one dirty habit I won't be picking up."

"Why don't we go walk it off?" Joe suggests.

"Yeah," Shmo says, glancing at Megan. "We should get her away from the smoky fire."

"Is that okay?" Megan asks Katy and me. "We'll just be gone a few minutes."

"Take your time," I tell them. "Katy and I can entertain ourselves."

"You're sure?" Zoey asks, slowly getting to her feet.

"Go."

As soon as the four of them are out of earshot, I tell Katy, "I thought they'd never leave. So tell me, tell me, tell me."

Katy suggests we go down by the water, so I follow her to a dry patch near the edge, and we sit. She proceeds to untie and tie the shoelaces of both her sneakers.

"C'mon, Katy. I'm not getting any younger."

"I'm just trying to think of how to say it."

"Would it help if I guess?"

"I don't know."

"All right. Let me try." I think for a minute and then ask, "Are you moving?"

She shakes her head.

"Thank god," I say. That had been my biggest fear. As much as I like Megan and Zoey, I would die if Katy left. I try another guess. "Are you doing drugs?"

"No."

"Did you steal something and get caught?"

"No."

"Are you pregnant?" I ask, laughing as I say it since I know that's not possible, unless Orlando is due for a virgin birth. But Katy isn't saying no. A tightness grips my chest and I grab her arm. "Katy, are you pregnant?"

"No, no, I'm not pregnant," she says.

I let out a deep breath. I've never been so happy to hear the word "no" before.

Then she adds, "It's pretty much the opposite of pregnant."

"Huh? What's the opposite of pregnant?"

She closes her eyes and says in a voice so soft I have to lean in to hear, "I have a crush on a teacher."

I laugh with relief. "Is that all? What's the big deal? You know I have a crush on Mr. Simon!"

"It's different," she says.

"Why is it different? Who is it, Principal Harrison? He's kinda old, but he's not bad looking, I guess."

She shakes her head and sighs. "It's Ms. Connors."

My jaw falls open. Katy reaches over and shuts it for me. My eyes are open so wide they feel too big for their sockets. Her words float out over the lake. I picture them hanging there, suspended in mid-air. My brains searches for things to say.

"But she's like . . . she's a . . . she's a woman," I stammer.

"I've noticed," Katy says, digging in the sand with a stick.

I still feel like I'm not hearing her correctly. Just to point out the obvious, I ask, "What about that time in the coat room in sixth grade when you kissed that kid Billy Something who moved to New Jersey?" My arms flail about in the air as I search for more examples of why Katy isn't gay. "Okay, and you went to second base with that boy you met at the Museum of Natural History last summer in New York. *Also,*" I continue, my voice rising, "Jeff Grand wanted to ask you to the prom before he found out sophomores can't ask people."

"He did?"

Even in the dark I can tell she's pleased. "Yes," I reply.

"Before this whole thing, I didn't think I was gay either," Katy says, jabbing the stick hard into the sand. "I'm very confused. I mean, I did like those two guys. And I even like Jeff Grand a little."

I stand up and sit back down for no good reason. I am very

aware that this is a hugely important conversation and I don't want to say anything stupid. I have to focus. I have to help her sort through this. It's like with the little girl at Disney this afternoon. It's so important to listen to the words between the words. The words that aren't being said. I lean back on my heels and ask, "Are you *attracted* to Ms. Connors? Like in a sexual way?"

She doesn't answer right away. Then she sighs and says, "I don't know. I look forward to her class every day. I like watching her teach. She's so free and confident and everything."

"It sounds like you admire her and want to be like her," I point out, hoping I'm not just grasping aimlessly. "Like I might admire Alyssa Levy's breasts, but I wouldn't want to kiss her."

She looks up at me. "That girl in our gym class?"

"You're missing the point."

"No, I get what you're trying to say. I hadn't thought of it that way before."

"But if you do want to kiss her," I begin, feeling this is an important point I need to get across, "if you do want to, then you can tell me."

"I'll have to think about that," Katy says. I wait for her to say more but she just sits there, lost in thought. At least her shoulders aren't hunched up anymore. Finally she says, "Thank you for being so cool about this. I was so scared to tell you."

"Don't be scared to tell me anything. I'm your best friend no matter what." Hey, if I can handle what happened with Dad today at Disney World, I can handle this.

"Aw, shucks," Katy says, in a southern drawl. "You're not gonna hug me now, are ya?"

"Very funny."

"It's weird," Katy says. "Now that two people know it doesn't seem like such a big deal."

"Are you serious? You told Ms. Connors you have a crush on her?" Oh, that can't have been good.

"No! Of course not," Katy says. "I mean you and Mrs. Lombardo in the school office. She read it in my note. You gave it to her this morning."

"What? No, I didn't! I gave your note back to you when you tackled me in the hall."

"No, you didn't. You gave me your mother's note excusing you from school. You gave *my* note to Mrs. Lombardo."

Once again, she shocks me. My jaw drops. I throw my hand over my mouth. "You're kidding me!"

"I kid you not."

I feel the laughter rising up from inside me and we both fall onto our backs in the sand. I laugh until my stomach aches.

In between giggles, Katy asks, "You don't think she'll tell Ms. Connors, do you?"

I shake my head, not even minding the sand that's now ground into my hair. "Mrs. Lombardo must have secrets on every kid in school. She's like a tomb."

"What are you guys laughing about?" Zoey says, approaching with Megan. I hadn't even heard them approaching. I hope they didn't hear anything else. Katy and I quickly stand up and brush the sand off ourselves.

Katy answers hurriedly, "An old *Seinfeld* rerun I watched last night when I couldn't fall asleep."

"Oh," Megan says. "I never really got that show."

Katy looks visibly relieved that they bought her excuse. She looks back and forth between the two of them and says, "So, it looks like you guys had a good time. Nice hickey, Megan."

Megan's hand flies up to her neck. The rest of us laugh.

"I wouldn't laugh, Zoey, if I were you," Megan says. "You have lipstick all over your chin."

Zoey frantically swipes at her chin with the sleeve of her sweatshirt.

"So where are Joe and Shmo?" I ask.

"Who?" Megan asks.

"Oh, sorry, I mean Marc and Justin."

"We sent them to hang with Dennis for a little while. It has to be just the four of us for this next part."

"Next part?" I ask. "Wasn't the blackberry brandy my birthday ritual?"

They all laugh, even Katy. "That was just to warm you up," Zoey says and plops down in the sand. The rest of us follow. "Ready?"

"As I'll ever be, I guess."

"Okay," Zoey says, leaning in toward me. "Truth or dare?"

"That's it?" I look around the circle. "Just truth or dare? That's easy." It's no contest. I always choose truth.

"You might want to hear what they are first," Megan warns. "Before choosing."

Zoey rubs her hands together, clearly enjoying this part. "Either you have to tell us the deepest, most secretive secret you know, or else you have to run into the lake naked."

I stare at her as she giggles with glee. "Naked!?" I demand. "Completely naked!?"

"Just your birthday suit," she says. "Hey, get it? It's actually your birthday!" The three of them laugh, but Katy's sounds forced. I'd bet anything she didn't know in advance what the truth option was going to be.

Fifteen minutes ago and I would have been so in the clear. I would have told them about stealing that rainbow-colored gel pen from Silverman's Cash 'n' Carry in seventh grade. Or that my father cried when he lost his job. Or that I saw Rob naked that time. But now I had a real secret. On the other hand, the lake is very dark and cold and slimy, and the thought of going in there is truly horrifying. That doesn't leave me much choice. I turn to Katy.

"Will you hold my clothes for me?"

She nods gratefully as I glance behind us to make sure the boys are far enough away. Then I pull off my jeans as Megan and Zoey begin shrieking.

"You're actually choosing *dare?*" Zoey shouts. "I can't believe it!"

"Oh my god," Megan says. "You're actually getting naked. You must have some huge secret!"

I've now pulled off my shirt and am standing there in my underwear. "Any chance you brought a towel?"

Zoey runs back to the bonfire, which by now is a lot lower since no one has tended it. She comes back with a hand towel.

"I never thought you'd choose Dare," she says. "I only bought this in case we spilled anything."

I grab the towel from her and use it as best I can to cover myself. With one push, my underwear falls to the ground. I drop the towel as close to the edge of the lake as possible.

"You can still change your mind," Zoey calls to me as I run into the very cold water.

The dare didn't say how far in I had to go, so I plan on only taking a few steps. But the shoreline is deceiving and I'm soon up to my thighs.

The three of them are cheering now. Katy calls out, "That's enough, Josie, come back."

As I turn around to go back my foot slips on a rock. I feel myself falling and know my bare butt is about to hit the bottom. My bare butt! I land just hard enough to alert me that no matter how hard I pretend, this isn't a part in a play. It's just me, in the lake, playing the only real role of my life. By the time I scramble upright, my hair is soaking wet and Katy is at my side, holding the towel. The water only comes up to the bottom of her knees.

"Thank you," she says, pressing the towel to me. "I owe you big time."

I shiver in response.

Zoey and Megan hug me when I get to shore, which I think is nice because I'm really wet, but on the other hand it's a little weird because I'm still naked. They hold out my clothes to me and turn around while I get dressed. I've never realized how difficult it is to put on jeans over wet legs. Katy and I still need to talk. She seems much more relaxed now than before she told me. So that's good, at least.

"You guys ready to go?" Dennis says, approaching from behind. I quickly pull my shirt over my head. I don't think he saw anything.

The four of them start back toward the fire pit as I bend down to pick up my sneakers and my bra, which I hadn't bothered to put back on. "Wait!" I call out frantically. Everyone stops. I hold up my left hand. "My ring is missing!"

They all hurry back except Dennis, who says he'll meet us at the car. "Where did you last see it?" Katy asks worriedly.

"On my finger. Before I went into the lake."

We turn to face the inky black water. "Oh, no," I say. "It's gone. My grandmother had it for fifty years and I had it for three hours!"

"Maybe it's in the sand," Megan suggests, kneeling down to look. "It could have fallen off when you took off your clothes."

We all get on our knees and feel around. "Does Rob still have that metal detector?" Katy asks.

"I think so." In his geek days Rob used to take his metal detector all over town. I went with him once to one of the manmade ponds on the outskirts of Disney World. After four hours of digging along the shore, all we found were three rusty nails, one nickel from 1976, an old high-heeled shoe, nine bottle caps, and a penny with the face completely burned off from the sun.

The four of us have come up empty, and I'm now on the verge of tears. "We'll never find it." The clouds keep blotting out the moon, and the beachfront is even darker now.

"Why don't we come back here early tomorrow morning," Katy suggests, scooping up handfuls of sand and letting it sift through her fingers. "It'll be much easier to search in the daylight."

I don't see any other choice. I nod miserably and reach for my sneakers. Putting wet, sand-covered feet in sneakers is totally unpleasant. Before I shove on my second one, I stop to shake out a pebble. Out falls my ring, right onto the sand.

"I found it!" I shout, holding it up high. My friends stop digging and look up. "It must have fallen in there when I pulled them off before." I stick the ring on my finger and promise myself to get it resized as soon as possible.

Megan stands up and brushes the sand off her knees. "Enough drama for one night, even for me."

We scurry back to the now only-sputtering fire to collect our stuff. "We should put the fire out," Zoey says. She looks around and sees the cups Katy and I left in the sand with the brandy still in them. She pulls one out of the sand and tosses the contents on the twigs. Then we all jump out of the way because instead of fizzling out, it flares up.

Katy says, "Didn't you pay attention in science class?" She scoops up sand and tosses it on the flames, eventually smothering them.

I pick up the brandy bottle to hand to Zoey, and am surprised to find it's empty. "Did you two drink all this?"

"Marc and Justin finished it," she says.

The only people left in sight are one smooching couple. "Where are those guys?" I ask.

"They must have taken off," Megan says, looking around. "Oh well. I didn't think Justin was going to be the love of my life anyway."

Zoey sighs. "Marc was a good kisser, though. Not too wet, not too dry. Not too hard, not too soft. That's okay, though. He's replaceable." She swings the backpack onto her shoulder and we head toward the path.

Dennis had thoughtfully pulled the car to the edge of the woods and turned on his headlights for us, so it is much easier to see this time. In the car we can't stop talking about what a crazy day this has been.

"I wonder what will happen in four years," Megan says. "On Josie's next Leap Day birthday."

"We probably won't all be together," Katy says quietly. "Zoey and I will be in college and you guys will be on Broadway or on TV or something. But probably not in Orlando."

That shuts us up for a minute as the reality of what she said sinks in. Then we pass the twenty-four-hour Circle K, and Megan points to it. "Dennis, can we stop?"

"What for?" he asks.

"You can't possibly be hungry after all the dessert we ate at Josie's," Zoey says.

I want to tell Zoey that if Megan wants to eat, we should all be encouraging her.

"All I want are mints," Megan replies. "I don't want my parents to smell the alcohol on my breath."

"That's a really good idea," Zoey says. "Dennis?"

"Oh, all right," he says, swinging the car into the parking lot. As usual, it's full, even at almost eleven on a Monday night.

No one wants to wait in the car, so we all go inside. The air conditioning is on full blast and I wish I had put my bra on after all. My wet hair hangs in cold strands down my back and I shiver. Megan heads toward the candy aisle and Katy and I wander through the magazines with all the pretty airbrushed models on the covers.

Making sure no one else is around, I ask, "Katy, do you want to come back to my house? We can continue our conversation and I can drive you back home. I can do that now, you know."

She shakes her head. "Thanks, but I just want to be alone to think."

Slightly hurt, I say, "Oh, okay," and pick up an issue of *Entertainment Weekly*. As I'm flipping through it, a guy's voice behind me says, "I guess you still want to be an actress."

I whirl around. Grant Brawner. What are the odds? He just keeps popping up where I least expect him. My stomach flips until I remember I'm mad at him. "Oh, it's you," I say. Katy silently slips away into the next aisle.

"I won't ask why you're all wet," he says.

"Good."

"Hey, I'm sorry about this afternoon. It was Stu's idea."

"Uh, huh."

"If it makes you feel any better, Stu and I are both out of the game. We got shot about ten minutes ago. Some girls got us right in front of the Slushee machine."

Actually, that does make me feel a little better. Just then his cell phone rings. He pulls it off his belt and looks at the number.

"It's my mother," he says apologetically, and answers it.

I pretend to keep reading the magazine.

"Yeah, it's me," he says into the phone. "Oh, really? What's her name?"

Is his mother trying to fix him up with someone? I really don't want to hear this. I slip the magazine back onto the shelf and rejoin my friends in front of the counter. Megan is flirting with Stu like nothing ever happened at my house. Traitor. She keeps pushing her hair in front of her neck to cover up evidence of Joe. Or Shmo. Whichever one she was with.

Grant finds us. "Bobby's baby was born a little while ago," he announces. "Her name is Amanda."

"I didn't know you were friends with him," I say, trying not to appear too interested in the whole baby thing, even though I am.

"I'm not, really," he says. Then he seems unsure. "Well, sort of, I guess."

"It seems to me," Zoey says, "that Sherri did all the hard work. You didn't even mention her."

Grant shrugs. "I'm sure she's fine."

Then I remember what Missy Hiver said at lunch. "They didn't break up, did they?"

"No."

I knew Missy was lying!

Megan pays for her mints and turns to Grant, still holding her hair in front of her neck even though Stu has wandered away. "I thought they were giving the baby up for adoption."

"They are," Grant says, pulling a piece of beef jerky out of the glass bowl on the counter.

"Then how come they named her?" Megan asks.

"I dunno."

"We've gotta go," Zoey tells us, glaring at Grant. "Dennis is already in the car."

Grant waits until we're halfway out the door to call out, "I'm really sorry about tricking you." We let the door close and run into the car laughing. As we pull away he's still watching us. I give a little wave goodbye. My obsession has passed. He's still totally hot, though.

Dennis drops me off first and waits at the curb as I stick the key into the front door. I'm about to turn it when Rob swings the door open. Since my hand is still on the keys I get yanked inside. He must have been waiting right there for me to get home. As soon as he sees me he starts laughing.

"So you chose *dare*, huh?"

"Yup." I step past him, accidentally sending a stray pack of Smarties rolling under the closet door.

"You must have a really good secret," he says, admiringly.

I nod. "I do."

"Because there are leeches in that lake, you know."

It takes a second for the words "leeches" and "lake" to come together in my brain. When they connect, I scream at the top of my lungs. Rob steps to the side, my parents run out of their room, and I run up the stairs and directly into my third shower of the day.

"Are you sure these girls are hot?" Justin asks his friend Marc as they toss another few twigs onto the growing fire. They've already piled rocks around the outside to protect it.

"I'm sure," Marc says. "I met one of them last week. She's a little pale, but hey, in the dark it doesn't matter, right?"

"That is correct, my man," Justin says, high-fiving Marc. They both take this opportunity to polish off their Coors Lights, which was the only kind of beer Marc could find in his older sister's fridge.

"Plus," Marc says, "she said she's bringing brandy."

"Sweet."

Marc nods. "I wish I could remember her name, though."

"Maybe another beer will help," Justin suggests.

Megan enjoys being outside late at night. It always feels like an adventure, even if she's only taking the trash out to the curb. She doesn't think real life offers enough adventure. That's why she is drawn to make-believe worlds and wants to be an actress. Megan likes putting on other people's lives like coats that she can slip on and off. She hopes tonight will prove to be an adventure. Maybe she'll even get some action with one of the guys from Orlando South.

As she follows a freaked-out Josie through the woods to the lake, Megan's sweatshirt pockets are weighed down with her share of the piñata candy. She also has the cigarettes she stole from Dennis's room. Before dinner, she had tried one in her bathroom. She blew the smoke out the window so her mother wouldn't smell it. For a few minutes the bitter taste it left in her mouth made her feel older. Then it just made her mouth taste gross and she had to brush her teeth twice. Plus everyone knows that smoking makes your skin gray and gives you even deeper lines on your face when you get older.

When she sees the guy intended for her she is psyched. He's preppier than the guys she usually likes, but he'll do fine for a one-night adventure.

Katy watches the square of chocolate sink to the bottom of her cup. Maybe getting drunk will make it easier to have The Conversation with Josie. Maybe it will fortify her. Take away her hesitancy and fears. Before she can change her mind, she lifts the cup to her mouth and takes a big gulp. In retrospect, she thinks that probably wasn't such a good idea. Her throat may never be the same again. When Megan and Zoey say they're going off with those two guys, she feels her chest tighten. The time has come and there's no getting out of it. Water always calms her, so she leads Josie to the edge of the lake. Watching the ripples of the water and the leaves drift by is almost like meditating. Usually, that is. Right now, it's barely having an effect.

Josie starts guessing and Katy almost hopes she lands on the right thing. That'll take away the pressure of having to actually say she might be gay. Or a lesbian. Or whatever a girl is called when she has a crush on another girl, or on a woman, in her case. Finally Katy sees her opening and she takes it. She holds her breath while Josie absorbs the news. At least Josie didn't storm off or say "That's gross" or anything. When Josie asks if she wants to kiss Ms. Conners, Katy pictures herself walking into the world religions classroom after school. Everyone has left for the day. Ms. Connors is sitting at her desk, slowly fanning herself with her hand because the air conditioning has broken. She looks up and says, "Hello, Katy. I was hoping you'd come see me." Then they walk toward each other, lean forward, and . . . and what? Katy can't see past that. Does this mean she doesn't want to kiss her? Or simply that her powers of imagination aren't strong enough?

When she and Josie laugh and fall down onto the sand, Katy is laughing more out of relief than anything else. Even if she doesn't figure this out right now, she is grateful that Josie will be by her side for the ride.

Megan can't help thinking that Justin's mouth tastes like barbecue sauce. At first she couldn't put her finger on what it was. But now she settles on barbecue sauce with medium spiciness. Barbecue sauce happens to be one of Megan's favorite condiments, but she prefers when it enters her mouth via fork. After a few minutes she gently turns her head to the side, not wanting to offend him. Now she's going to need a mint to take the taste out of her mouth. Justin takes her move as a sign that she wants him to kiss her neck. All she thinks while he's doing it is that it's going to leave a bruise.

Zoey glances through the trees at Megan and Justin. Justin is kissing Megan's neck, and Megan has her eyes closed. Marc is talking about some big golf tournament in town next weekend, so of course she stopped listening almost immediately. She feels bad that Katy and Josie don't have anyone to be with. It would have been really cool to set up Josie on her birthday, and Katy could use a little action too. While Marc is yammering on about "below par" and "a Big Bertha" — which she thinks is a kind of golf club but isn't really sure — an old memory is sliding around the outskirts of Zoey's brain. Something about the way Marc kisses reminds her of someone else, but she can't quite place it.

Megan and Justin step out from behind the trees and join them. "We should go," Megan tells Zoey. "Katy and Josie must be wondering where we are."

Zoey agrees and tells the boys they have to go sit with Dennis for the next ten minutes. She tells them Dennis is an old friend, because she's too embarrassed to admit that her brother had to come along. When the boys try to argue she leans in and kisses Marc on the lips. "Just ten minutes," she says. When they walk away, she says to Megan, "Boys are so easy."

At first when they return to the bonfire, they think Katy and Josie must have left.

"Oh my god," Megan says. "We're the worst friends in the world.

We just ditched them for some stupid guys. And it's Josie's Leap Day birthday!"

"Calm down," Zoey says. "There they are, by the water." She watches as Katy and Josie fall back onto the sand. "They seem just fine."

"Oh. Okay. Good."

As they head toward them, Zoey suddenly stops and says, "Greg Adler."

"Huh?"

"Greg Adler, summer after sixth grade, seven minutes in the closet."

"The kid who's having his bar mitzvah at fifteen? What about him?"

"I was trying to think of who Marc reminded me of."

"Marc isn't anything like Greg." Megan says. "Greg is shorter and has dark hair."

"Not their looks, the way they kiss."

"You remember a kiss from sixth grade?"

"You never forget your first kiss. I think I may give Greg another shot. If Marc doesn't call, of course."

"Of course," Megan says.

Katy is stunned when she hears Zoey ask Josie the Truth or Dare question. Her heart feels like it has stopped beating as she waits for Josie's answer. Why couldn't she just have waited to tell Josie her secret until after the initiation was over? Then Josie would have such an easy choice. There's no way Josie is going into that cold, dark lake naked.

When Josie starts silently taking off her clothes, the wave of gratitude that Katy feels is like nothing she's ever experienced. She decides then and there that she will do whatever it takes to make sure Josie knows how much her act of self-sacrifice means to her.

Dennis tosses a handful of sand onto his small fire and heads toward his sister and her friends, who are at the edge of the lake. His last exchange with Marc and Justin had gone like this:

Justin (to Marc): Dude, you were right. They were total hotties. I like a girl with a few extra curves.

Marc: I think mine is a sure thing. That red hair is such a turn-on.

Dennis: Do you even know their names?

Blank looks from both.

Dennis: If you don't leave right now I'll tell them every word you just said.

Marc: So?

Dennis: And then I'll kick your butts all over town.

Justin: Dude, you're not that scary.

Dennis had a trick up his sleeve. He stood up and gave them the look that he'd practiced for hours in front of the bathroom mirror. The look said, *You better start running, because I just may be psycho.*

So now Dennis is coming alone to tell the girls it's time to go. He sees Josie walk out of the water with something held in front of her that's not doing a very good job covering anything. The trees are casting a shadow over most of the lakefront, so he doesn't think she can see him. He turns away anyway, just in case. He's already seen enough. In the moonlight she had seemed to him to be carved out of a smooth piece of ivory. Like an ancient chess piece. He likes how her body isn't perfectly proportioned. It's so much more real than those pictures under his bed. He waits until she's fully dressed (well, almost) until he approaches them.

While the rest of them look for Josie's ring, Dennis hurries back to the car, feeling a little guilty about seeing what he saw, even though it wasn't on purpose. He repositions the car and turns on the brights so Josie won't be so scared on the way back. It's the least he can do. That summer he will write a poem about a girl and a lake that wins fifty dollars. When the prize money arrives, he will use a tiny bit of rubber cement to stick a twenty-dollar bill onto the windshield of Josie's car, so when she finds it in the morning she'll think it blew there. Unfortunately, it is Rob who finds it and celebrates by buying himself a new CD and one of those plastic gizmos that make it easier to open the CD wrapper.

Ten hours after her water broke, Sherri delivers a healthy baby girl with ten fingers and ten toes. It hurt less than she had expected, but she knows the drugs helped. The doctor makes sure she is doing all right and then rushes out for an emergency C-section down the hall. The nurse cleans the baby off and lays her on Sherri's chest. Bobby kneels by the side of the bed and touches the baby's cheek.

"What are you going to name her?" the nurse asks.

"Amanda," Sherri says definitively. Bobby doesn't answer at all.

Another nurse then rushes in and whispers something to the first one. Together they pick up the baby.

"I'm so sorry, honey," the first nurse says when Sherri reaches out for the pink bundle. "I didn't know the situation."

The baby starts to cry as she is taken from the room. The pain Sherri feels now is much worse than the delivery itself. But she and Bobby don't change their minds. For that, Hayley and David Solomon of North Miami Beach are forever grateful. In eighteen years the baby will have the right to contact her birth parents. But she won't.

"We could win this whole thing," Stu says to Grant as they stroll through the aisles of the Circle K. "Five hundred bucks. That'd be so sweet."

"Not if we keep running in here every hour for chocolate. You're like a girl." Grant turns the corner and runs straight into Stacey Lu, a girl in his study hall. She just moved here last year and is a total hottie. He's never spoken to her before.

"Is being like a girl so bad?" she asks with a wicked smile.

"I'll answer that," Stu says, pushing Grant out of the way. "Being like a girl is an excellent thing. Especially when they look like you."

"Are you just saying that so I won't shoot you?" She reaches for her

Nerf gun at the same moment Stu pulls his out of his jacket pocket. They face off, both grinning, neither moving.

Stacey's equally hot teammate, Randi Gold, comes up behind them. "Uh, guys. I don't think a convenience store is the best place to be waving guns at each other, fake or not."

"They're orange," Stu says. "I don't think anyone's going to mistake them for real."

"No, she's right," Stacey says. "I'll lower mine if you do."

"C'mon, man," Grant says, nervously eyeing the security mirrors.

"Okay," Stu concedes. "But no funny business."

Stacey nods and at the same time they slowly lower their guns to their sides.

"So, what do we do now?" Stu asks. "We're trapped here together. As soon as one of us makes a move we'll all get shot. We'll both lose. Unless . . ."

"Unless what?" Randi asks.

"Unless you guys strip down. Then we won't be able to shoot you."

Grant laughs. He's gotta hand it to Stu. He's always thinking.

"Or you could just let us shoot you," Randi suggests, stroking her long blonde hair with one hand. Grant wants to reach out and stroke it, but of course he doesn't.

"Now why would we want to do that?" Stu asks, leaning one arm against the Slushee machine.

"Because, as you said, otherwise we'll all lose. But if you let us take you out of the game, we'll go out with you Saturday night."

"Even if you don't wind up winning in the end?" Grant asks.

"Yup," Stacey promises. "Right, Randi?"

Randi nods, still playing with her hair.

Grant pulls Stu aside. "So? Whaddaya think?"

"I don't know, man. Five hundred bucks."

"We have no idea if we're really gonna win," Grant points out. "Thirty teams are still alive out there. And some of them have grudges."

Stu turns back to the girls, who are waiting patiently, clicking their nails on the counter. "We'll want your phone numbers first."

The girls agree, and Stacey scribbles them on the back of an old receipt. She hands it to Grant, who looks it over and sticks it in his pocket, satisfied.

"Okay," Grant says. "We're ready to be sacrificed." As he waits for the dart to hit him, he pats his pocket. He has a backup plan in case the girls gave fake phone numbers or break the date. Stacey's credit card number is on the receipt from Banana Republic she just gave him. That could go a long way toward softening the blow.

Rob finishes his homework and checks his watch for the tenth time in as many minutes. He can't be expected to focus on his homework when Anne ignored his phone message and his sister is in a car with the kid known around school as Dennis the Menace. When he goes off to college next year, who is going to look out for her? He goes to the bathroom to splash water on his face. As he reaches for the hand towel he hears his parents talking animatedly in their room. He puts his ear up to the air vent so he can hear them better.

"Mumble mumble Disney World mumble mumble help people mumble."

Rob figures his mother must have opened the folder on the dresser and discovered Dad's new job. He checks his watch again. Where is Josie, already? Rob grabs his bag of piñata candy from the floor of his room, goes downstairs, and plops down on the last step. As he sits there watching the door, he polishes off four Tootsie Rolls, a box of watermelon-flavored Nerds, and two grape Pixy Stix. With football season over and no girlfriend, he figures he's allowed to comfort himself with junk food.

Finally a car door slams shut outside. Rob jumps to his feet and tosses his candy bag in the den to hide the evidence. Once he hears Josie's key in the door he swings it open and she comes flying in. He can't believe it when he sees her wet hair. He would have sworn on his life that she would never have gone in that water. Clearly she is braver than she used to be. He'll need to remember that. The mention of leeches sends her over the edge, though.

As he goes into the den to retrieve his candy, he realizes that, mixed in with the musty lake smell that Josie emitted as she ran past him was the distinct aroma of peppermint. That could only mean one thing. He runs up the stairs and knocks hard on the bathroom door. The shower is already running.

He gets no answer, so he knocks again, harder. He hisses through the door, "Josie Taylor! Have you been drinking?" He doesn't want to call out too loudly and bring their parents into the hall again.

But Josie doesn't hear him, either. She is too busy scrubbing every inch of her body. She scrubs places she didn't know she could reach. She pays special attention to the places that had never, before tonight, been exposed to the outdoors. She washes her hair twice. It's a good thing there isn't a drought right now, because Josie uses enough water to fill the dolphin pool at SeaWorld. Finally satisfied that she is leech-free, she dries off and pulls on her robe. She uses the hair dryer to dry her hair but doesn't bother putting any effort into straightening it. She's just going to sleep on it anyway. Then she opens the bathroom door and trips right over Rob, who for some unknown reason is sleeping outside the door.

Chapter 12: Josie Gets the Last Word

"Put up your right hand and swear you only had one sip," Rob says as we both scramble to get up from the floor.

I raise my hand. "I swear. May I go to my room now?"

"You may. Hey, wait. Do you think Katy Parker would go out with me?"

I stare at him like he just spoke in Chinese. "Katy? As in, my best friend Katy?"

"Would it be weird?"

I cannot find the words to respond.

"Yeah," he says, "it would probably be too weird. Forget I mentioned it. Sorry for nearly killing you on your birthday."

He doesn't know I can't die on my birthday, and I don't bother to tell him. He also doesn't know just how weird it truly would be if I asked Katy if she wanted to date Rob right now. And I'm CERTAINLY not going to tell him why.

Back in my room I slip on the red silk pajamas. They feel amazing next to my rubbed-raw skin. I check myself out in the full-length mirror inside my closet door. I look older. More sophisticated. Like an old-time movie actress in some black-and-white movie. I pull my hair into a ponytail and then push everything off my bed in one fell swoop. My books, pens, hair clips, lipstick tubes, birthday presents all go flying. It seems like something one of those dramatic actresses would have done. As soon as everything crashes down, I realize it was stupid. I'm lucky the sunglasses Rob gave me didn't break. I put them in my bookbag so I'll have them tomorrow for when I drive myself to school. Rob offered to get a ride with someone so I could take my friends. Jason Count and his girlfriend-whose-name-starts-with-an-E will just have to snuggle without us watching them.

I lay down on my bed, luxuriating in the feel of the silk on my skin. Grandma was right. Every sixteen-year-old should have a pair of these. Especially after she's jumped naked into a cold, slimy, leech-infested lake. Only now does it really sink in that I was naked in front of not only my friends, but also whoever else may have been lurking around. Thinking of being naked reminds me of what I had intended as my last activity of the night. I sit up and open the night-table drawer. BREAST BOOST . . . FULLNESS AND GROWTH. GUARANTEED! We'll just see about that.

I unbutton my pajama top and stand in front of the full-length mirror. The directions tell me to rub a pea-sized amount onto both breasts. How do I know what qualifies as pea-sized? Sometimes Mom gives us those little dark green peas with dinner, and sometimes the peas are bright green and, like, twice as big. Well, if bigger is better I might as well go for the bigger pea. Plus, I don't even need to use it on both breasts. I just want to catch the right one up with the left one. I squeeze a glob of the purple goo onto my fingers. Here goes. With the recommended circular motion, I massage the goo onto its intended target. The goo is supposed to rub all the way in, but after the allotted full minute of massaging, my skin still feels sticky. If Mom talks to her plants to make them grow, maybe I should try that.

"Grow. Enlarge thyself. Take up more space in my bra." Okay. I officially feel like an idiot and hope no one heard that. For the next thirty minutes I run back and forth from the mirror to my desk, where I make a halfhearted attempt to do my homework. At least I breezed right through those seven deadly sins. I may even have made up a few new ones not on the list.

Three minutes later: No change.

Five minutes later: Still no change.

Eight minutes later: Slight redness appears.

Twelve minutes later: Redness fades to pinkness.

Fifteen minutes later: Is the bottom half puffier?

Twenty minutes later: Bottom half definitely puffier. Looks weird.

Twenty-five minutes later: Still smaller than other one.

Twenty-eight minutes later: Still smaller, still pinkish.

Twenty-nine minutes later: Sort of puffy, sort of swollen, think it may be my imagination.

Thirty minutes later: I am in the bathroom washing it off. If any of my birthday wishes had to *not* come true, I'm glad it was this one.

Back in my room I shut off the light and slide between the sheets. I may never go back to regular pajamas again. I stare up at the ceiling, not ready to shut my eyes. I hope Katy doesn't regret that she told me her secret. I hope I didn't say anything too stupid. Maybe I should have told her I think Ms. Connors is pretty too. That probably wouldn't have come out right.

Two seconds later I swing my legs off the side of the bed and spring up. How could I have forgotten to check for the play postings? Mr. Polansky said they'd be up by midnight and it's five minutes till. Not even bothering to turn on the light, I drum my fingers on the desk as I wait for the modem to connect. The glow of the computer screen illuminates something pink lying halfway under the bed. I reach down and pick up the thin candle that Mom had included in the box with her muffins. It must have fallen out of my pants when I swept everything off my bed. My birthday still isn't officially over, so I figure I should be allowed one last birthday wish. Rather than finding something to stick it in, I hold the candle in my left hand and light a match with my right. Not an easy task, but like I said, I'm a good balancer. This morning my wish would have been a no-brainer. I would have wished that when the postings came up, next to the role of Juliet would be my name. But now my wish is different. I hold the candle in front of my face and close my eyes.

"I wish that whatever I find when the list comes up is exactly the way it's supposed to be." I open my eyes and blow out the candle. The Web site has come up. The link for the list is right there, blinking on and off. I take a deep breath and click on it.

The first word I see is *Juliet*. And next to *Juliet* is . . . *Stephanie Rose*. Stephanie. Not Josie. I close my eyes and lean back in my chair. I wait to feel the crushing blow, but it doesn't come. I'm too brain-dead from this incredibly long, bizarre day to analyze why. Stephanie must be one of the seniors. This would be her last chance to be in a school play. This morning that wouldn't have mattered to me. I take another deep breath, open my eyes, and scan down the list for my name. There I am, Josie Taylor, right next to the words *Lady Capulet*. At least I got a main role. I guess Mr. Polansky thinks I'm mature enough to play an older woman. I guess I must be if I don't feel like curling into the fetal position and crying over losing Juliet. The next name on the list is *Juliet's Nurse*. Megan got the part! I turn off my monitor and slide back into bed. Too bad Megan didn't try harder. She would have made a great Juliet.

I close my eyes and then toss my extra pillow onto the floor in preparation for where I'll end up in the morning. I have the same thought every four years when my Leap Day birthday ends — tomorrow will be March 1st. Just a regular day, where I'll be no one special. Absolutely nothing will separate me from anyone else. But this time something's different. This time, I don't believe it.